Praise for *Tia*

'From the very first paragraph, I found myself glued to every page wanting to reach out to the characters. The beautiful description of each location landed me there as if I was back in the early nineties myself in Dublin and Cork. I couldn't but help think of my own family whilst turning each page.'

— Pat Shortt

'A tender, beautifully written book about memory, secrets and marriage. The writing is gorgeous: cliché-free and simple without being basic. The characters feel real, and I really liked the use of poetry and lyrics. Although the story moves back and forward, I never lost the thread of where I was and what was happening. I know this can be very difficult to achieve.'

— Rachael English

'Brilliantly observed. A superb piece of work. All the place history and song references really worked. The Cork setting was masterly. It reminded me – in a good way – of Bernard MacLaverty's *Midwinter Break*.'

— Joe Duffy

'If you have ever been a partner to someone suffering the indignities and sadness of dementia – and even if you haven't – this is a heart-breaking and must-read story, told with honesty and compassion.'

— Steph Booth

'In this elegiac, finely observed novel, Vignoles has produced a tender, exploration of memory, identity and love as a man descends into early onset Alzheimer's disease. The disease's ambiguities are skilfully evoked with a series of resonant, finely observed, vignettes. Long-buried memories are unearthed, past secrets and mistakes return as he and his wife come to understand how this transformative event requires them to acknowledge the new needs of a rapidly changing life.'

– Sarah Harte

TIDES GO OUT

A Novel

JULIAN VIGNOLES

ORPEN PRESS

Published by
Orpen Press
Upper Floor, Unit B3
Hume Centre
Hume Avenue
Park West Industrial Estate
Dublin 12

email: info@orpenpress.com
www.orpenpress.com

Paperback ISBN 978-1-78605-162-2
ePub ISBN 978-1-78605-163-9

The characters and events in this book are fictional. Any resemblance to actual events or persons, living or dead, is entirely coincidental.

Printed in Dublin by SPRINTprint Ltd

In memory of Rodney Rice

'When I was younger, I could remember anything, whether it had happened or not; but my faculties are decaying now and soon I shall be so I cannot remember any but the things that never happened.'

– Mark Twain

Prologue

Fiona heard pencil scraping paper and felt a chill. The doctor had asked her husband, Con, to draw a clock. She looked on, shocked at the effort it took to produce a bumpy-looking circle.

He sighed, looked sadly at the paper, then at the doctor.

'Now, can you fill in the numbers that correspond to the hours?'

Con stared at the paper and wrote '12' at the top, then hesitated before putting '11' just to the left of it. He continued adding the other numbers and made it a little unevenly to the '1', though it was too far away from the '12'.

'Now, could you draw hands on the clock, to tell the time of ten past eleven?'

Con scrunched up his face and looked at Fiona. 'Simple. It should be so simple,' he kept saying.

The doctor was matter of fact. 'This test is used a lot because it assesses several cognitive areas that dementia effects, what's called executive function, motor programming, and attention and concentration.'

She barely heard the words, the dreaded one too. Her mind wandered; scenes flashed by as a lump came to her throat.

Images of their life together, the harmony she took for granted swirled through a kaleidoscope. Her world was tumbling around her.

1

2019

Cork comes in and out of focus as Con makes his way along St Patrick's Street. Buses come and go, engines rev, brakes hiss, people wait, destinations glow in LED: Blackpool, Ballyphehane, Wilton. He nods expectantly at people. *How's it going?* They just smile politely, look down or turn away. *Do I know that lad from somewhere?*

He doesn't look dapper or purposeful – a tweed jacket pulled over the t-shirt he slept in, days as a sharply dressed man behind him. He looks around before taking a quick swig from a naggin of Jameson. It confirms the fiery liquid's age-old appeal. He slips the bottle back into a pocket. The drink is a help – to try and forget what had happened that morning, what Fiona found.

A breeze brings salty air up the river. The weight of a camera bag nags him. He's grown weary of something he'd agreed to do in the aftermath of the diagnosis: a video diary – reality-TV-style, to document the effects of the disease, to record his own decline. Some instinct from that old life leapt across the damaged neural pathways, so he's taken the bag with him leaving the house. He tugs the camera out and places it on the bridge. Pressing RECORD, he takes a few steps back and stares into the lens.

'I've been strolling through the city for the last … hour or so …'

The breeze makes the camera wobble a little on the parapet. He's sure a seagull is giving him a dirty look, so he glowers back until the creature cries out, spreads its wings, and takes off over the silently moving Lee. Con continues:

'I see places I don't really recognise. I just feel like … there's a monster out to get me, not like one under the bed when I was little. This one's much closer, like somewhere inside my head …'

Turning around, he looks vacantly down river, watching a ship leave a berth and move slowly on its way. Something makes him recall an evening walk by the harbour in Copenhagen, a ferry to Stockholm manoeuvring close by, a ship's horn sounding, swirling water, salt in the air, the romance of the sea calling. He was with somebody. Fiona? No, her hair was different, her aura mysterious. A lover? The scene fades.

He stares around him before spotting the camera, picks it up without turning it off and puts it back in the bag, where it continues its low hum.

At the bottom of Winthrop Street, he sees the door of the Long Valley. Flashes of memory come – clinking glasses, laughter, casual conversation with strangers.

A quiet pint won't do any harm.

He walks in, reassured by a convivial hum.

'Con!' says a voice.

Who's that? He tries hard to match the face with the surroundings. Something flashes.

'Liam!'

He knows him from bars, mainly. A decent bass player, he'd gigged with several bands over the years. They dropped him, one by one. He wasn't reliable, not even for a band on the fringe of the Cork scene. Porter was the main cause, but mental health was an issue too.

'You'll have a pint, boi?' says Liam.

Liam's grubby woollen jumper has stains so ancient that their original colour is lost to memory, but Con's brain doesn't register such things nowadays. All he sees is a familiar face.

Soon Con's drink of choice is in front of him, a creamy Beamish, and he watches it settle.

'How's it going, lad?' asks Liam.

'Eh … I'm having a wander around town.'

'Are ye not busy making telly programmes?'

What's he on about? Telly … Con puts the glass to his lips.

'Weren't you producing for years?' Liam asks.

'Eh … that was then … this is now, I suppose … as the fella said,' Con wheezes.

A drinkers' interval. Then Liam looks at the bag and asks what's in it.

'It's … a little camera. Have you ever seen one like this?' Con says, taking it out and placing it on the counter, the lens facing them, the camera still recording since the time he'd taken it out at the bridge.

'You're on telly now!' Con says.

Another pause. A clock ticks.

'I'm in a bit of trouble with my wife,' Con says.

His companion is startled but doesn't let on. 'What is it exactly? Is she due to meet you here, boi, and she's late?'

'I don't think so.'

'So, what is it?'

'It's just that …' Con struggles to express what has come into his head.

'I know. She's seen you with a young one, Con?' Liam teases.

Con just stares. Liam hopes for a salacious reveal, but instead Con downs his pint, slams the glass back hard on the counter, and slides off the stool to his feet.

'Are you off, boi? Here, what about that yoke?'

Con grabs the camera, this time switching it off, just about managing to put it in the bag and get the straps around his shoulders.

He walks along Oliver Plunkett Street. Talk of television has stirred something. Pictures from his old life are coming back – the routine of cameras, lights, professional tensions, little jealousies. He struggles to order his thoughts. Once a memory surfaces, there seems no way to control how vivid it gets. Now he's back in a hotel room, bed linen thick and soft, furtive passion, tender murmurings. Who is she? Where were they?

He hears a voice call his name. He can't find a face in the noise, the people on errands, workers rushing back from a lunch that had gone on, sandwiches being eaten on the move, or a sneaky rendezvous ending with a quick kiss of promise, the clang of porter kegs being delivered, people passing judgement on nice things in windows.

'Con Twomey ...' the voice comes again.

It's the man's prominent nose that Con recognises. That was it: they'd sat together several times in front of screens in a TV control room, Con barking instructions to camera people over a talkback. A million years ago.

Con's expression makes the man draw back, fidget with his coat, start to walk on. Con creases his face; that man had done him a bad turn once, he's sure; there'd been an incident on a programme, though he can't recall what or when. A bad feeling lingers as the man disappears.

In The English Market, he savours the aroma of cheese and bread before it's overtaken by salty air. A stall holder in a white coat looks his way. A whole salmon on ice is on display. The slimy scales glisten as Con scrutinises it, the sea smell making him think of fishing with the kids on a pier somewhere one summer. Something makes him pick up the creature, surprised by how heavy and slippery it is. People stare. He struggles with it, before letting go. It makes a thump on the tiled floor. Pieces of ice skid to the feet of passers-by. A woman screams.

'What the …?' someone shouts.

A man picks up the lifeless fish and places it back on the counter before the stall holder gets to Con.

He finds the exit onto Grand Parade, negotiates the pedestrian crossing, and wanders through Bishop Lucey Park. Coming to a gate, he sees the wall of Ziggy's Bar. Inside, a familiar greeting: 'A pint of the usual?'

A loud American is holding court, taken with the pub's interior – a sort of shrine, pictures of rock legends in their glory days, Phil Lynott, Rory Gallagher, and Status Quo, caught in youthful swagger, the fading glimpses of stellar careers still inviting remembrance.

'But buddy … of your living greats,' the American drones, 'it's hard to beat Van Morrison. You know –'

'Turn it up!' Con shouts, startling everyone. Music is playing in his head. He abandons the conversation and waltzes out of the pub into the evening – to the sound of bass and drums. He kicks the air, stumbling along South Main Street. The reeds vibrating in the saxophones encourage him onwards.

'Turn it up!' he roars.

At South Gate Bridge, he stops dead. Heavy rain is falling. He doesn't care and just stares; the river below had always been such a part of his life. Childhood memories come; Patrick Galvin set a poem at this bridge, one about his father's decline, 'My Father Spoke with Swans'. 'Why', the teacher asked them all those years ago, 'did the poet's father want to communicate with the swans?' *'Was it because he was going mad, Sir?' That's what I said to the teacher that day.*

Soaking wet, he takes the bag from his shoulder and places it on the parapet. He needs to get a raincoat but struggles with the task. A breeze catches the coat as he tries to put it on. His confusion grows. The sound of rain falling on plastic irritates him, the water below seems menacing now. He doesn't notice the bag slipping from the stone till his eye catches it tumbling in slow motion towards the water. Reacting slowly, he can only stare as it hits the Lee channel, the current taking it swiftly under the bridge. It was all too much to handle – the rain, the wind, night closing in, his brain in meltdown. *The camera! What happened to it?*

In panic he runs to the other side of the bridge. Is there a way down to the water's edge? The rain, the dark, the turmoil in his head – things are getting out of hand. A car horn nearly deafens him. The incident at home that morning rages in his mind. People shout at him to mind the cars. He stops. He can see Fiona waving something at him – frowning.

'What's this, Con?'

He stared at her. It was coming back – the aura of another, her scent, the tone of a whispered voice, her use of English. Yes, it was a hotel room. When, where?

He just keeps walking into the dusk.

2

Fiona paused under the sculpted arms of Christ that framed the entrance, pushed open the oak door and savoured the hush. It was her place to reflect, where the volume of the world – and Cork city – could be turned down for a while. She never tired of the symbolism of that entrance: the strong arms of Our Lord protecting those who passed, looking out for those who didn't, too. The emphatic concrete shapes suggested fervour to her, a motive to face life – the good and the bad.

The church also brought refuge from what happened that morning.

She wore her favourite wool coat, a denim skirt, and flat shoes. She wasn't a flashy dresser, though she liked a little makeup sometimes: today it was a light red lipstick that gave just the right amount of emphasis to her lips. She was fifty-seven. Her long black hair, with some unwelcome grey advancing, was tied up casually with a woollen band.

Maybe there was an innocent explanation for the hotel receipt she'd found. 'It's a receipt for a *double room*, Con!'

He'd looked at her helplessly. He wasn't well – so should she just forget about it?

She bowed her head and whispered a prayer. It was the second anniversary of her mother's death. Black and white scenes from her childhood, footage of happy birthday parties and smiling parents flickered in her imagination. Did I repay their love? It was the time they kept asking what she was going to do after college, when she seemed to be aimless.

The church door opened, and a man walked past her to another pew, to kneel in prayer. It still had meaning for some. What was it that caused *him* to seek solace here? Did he, like her, feel a need for the love and help of a Supreme Being, whom we know as Jesus Christ? Were they both clinging to something from another age? Most of her friends, apart from one or two who attended weekly Mass, had little need for religion. Did they ever wonder why *she* had?

She said a silent prayer for her children, Ciarán and Nóra. She loved them, was proud of them, though often wished they'd more time for belief – like hers. In the silence she whispered a special prayer. It brought memories back, of a time before she met Con, the year of that rediscovery of prayer. Her younger self walked carefree through Trinity College, books and lecture notes in a shoulder bag, her hair untidier than it was now, her jeans tight, her top baggy. She was sitting with a mug of coffee when someone called her name. It was another student, James. He was leaning back in his chair, hands behind his head, long legs stretched out in macho pose.

'I saw you at the lecture,' he said.

She liked him, despite the strutting; he was part of a gang that drank regularly in O'Neill's pub close by. Sitting close to him one night as inebriation set in, she enjoyed the accidentally-on-purpose way his thigh rubbed against hers once or twice. A few weeks later they were in America together. But the memory of all that was sour.

Her earlier upset abated, and now she worried about Con. The doctor warned that more and more brain functions would go, like the ability to react appropriately to others. 'How complex our brains are,' he said, talking about all the billions of nerve cells linked to one another. 'There are trillions of pathways in there. It's a wonder it works so well so much of the time.'

Was she right to confront him earlier? He could have left the house and be out and about, having one of those non-conversations with someone, making a fool of himself, or worse.

She stood up and genuflected. Outside, she wrapped her scarf tightly around her face. In the twilight, the church lights illuminated a descending shower of sleet. It swirled in the glow, creating a slow-motion effect, taking her mind briefly off her troubles. She kept walking towards home, oblivious to the wind that blew in gusts around her, the roar of cars and buses, consumed with her thoughts.

3

She kept going out to the front gate, hoping to see Con's familiar form stumbling towards her. Incoherent – drunk even – she didn't care. Where was he?

Feck him!

She made phone calls, drank tea, took deep breaths, worry growing, feeling a mixture of anger, guilt, and dread. Other evidence came to mind: a postcard from years before, a picture from a Greek beach and the message, 'You'd love it here, x.'

Happier memories wouldn't go away. A night in Dublin in 1993.

'That fella keeps gawking at you,' said her friend Deirdre. They and another pal, Emma, were on a night out at a gig in Whelan's. The band's front man, all three agreed, was a bit of a heartthrob.

'Good band?' the stranger said, leaning close. It was an old chat-up line, but there was something appealing about him – tall, a nice smile, and well-turned-out, she decided, after glancing him up and down.

'A new friend there?' Emma winked.

After the last encore and the lights came up, but she didn't want this man to disappear. She gave the girls a wide-eyed look and a quick wink.

'See you so, Fiona,' they said in unison, grinning as they slipped away.

'Would you fancy a drink?' he asked, as the crew started moving gear around. He seemed earthy, maybe dashing in his own way.

When he told her he was from Cork, she said she'd never been there.

'You haven't seen much of the world, then?'

'I wouldn't quite say that.'

She told him she was a Dubliner, living with her parents in Clontarf, an only child. She'd done Arts in Trinity and worked as a secondary school teacher. 'I've had a fairly comfortable life, I suppose.'

'Were you a wild one in your student days at all?' he ventured.

'In a way, yes.' It was a part of her life she'd put behind her, but on a whim, she thought it might impress him. 'I had my wilder days, yes,' she said nervously.

'Boyfriends?'

'One or two.'

She didn't want to sound sheltered or dull. 'I did a mad thing the summer I finished college. I took off to the States with a fella. It was an impulsive thing. Adventurous, too, I suppose. He was a bit of a Blues fanatic. We worked for a bit, headed south, and ended up in Mississippi. But the relationship, well … it started to unravel.'

'You and this fella were …?'

'Getting on each other's nerves in the end, yes. Can you imagine how hot it was there in August?'

She couldn't elaborate – on the scorching weather and cooling relations, the terrible feeling of being in a strange place with someone who'd become almost alien to her. But she could never forget. After another night in a cheap, stifling hotel, she was on her way home – traumatised – to Dublin and its certainties.

'So, where's this lad nowadays?' Con said, lifting his pint again.

'I haven't a clue,' she said, her mind wandering.

He changed the subject. 'Well, you can't take the Corkman out of me. I've never strayed far, city-born and bred. But I'm in exile now.'

He told her about his roots in Fair Hill on the northside of the city and his parents' determination to get him a place in University College Cork.

'I did Music, now I work in television – for my sins.'

She gleaned he'd dabbled in concert promotion after qualifying and made a documentary about the Cork music scene. It had technique, pace and plenty of irreverence, a reviewer said. Then he got a job as a producer/director in RTÉ. She was interested in all that: she didn't have any friends who worked in media. But the appeal for her at that moment was a sense that this man was confident, yes, but gentle, too – not the macho man she'd once fallen for; she'd got things so wrong ten years before, when she was too impressionable. Could this quiet feeling now lead to happiness?

The evening of their first date, Con was at the bus stop as the number 15 approached Rathmines, where he was renting a flat. Soon he was pointing out the red sandstone town hall, then the Art Deco-style post office. 'There's a little New York glamour about this place. A legend – like Bob Dylan – could step out and you'd bump into them in the doorway …' He laughed.

A man with imagination, she concluded, seeing a more functional-looking building. She wasn't given to flights of fancy like that, but it was endearing.

'What do you know about Cork?' he asked her, watching her lips disappear into the head of a pint of Smithwick's in Slattery's pub.

'Cork? Well … there's Seán Ó Ríordáin, the poet, for starters,' she said.

'Good.'

'Wait, I'm the teacher here,' she laughed, putting down her glass. She felt this was more than casual – could this man be special? On the second pint, her imagination began to test her; what would it be like if he kissed her? Should *she* make a move? What if she did and he rejected her? She searched for clues; intimacy must have been on his mind, otherwise they could have met in the city centre and not around the corner from where he lived. *No, just drinks.*

An hour and a half later, she paused and reached for her bag.

'That was good, but two's my limit. I'd better head northside.'

She was glad Con didn't seem disappointed as they waited for a city-bound bus.

'Good to see you again,' he said as her bus pulled up.

'And you.'

Staring at the lights of Dublin from the bus, she thought about how she'd longed for a man. Was this him?

'What's the Cork fella like?' Deirdre wanted to know when they met in Bewley's two days later.

'I like him.'

'Careful, Fiona. What's different about *this* fella?'

'I'm not sure, but I've a very good feeling about him.'

Deirdre touched her arm. 'I'm glad.'

Fiona liked the way Deirdre blew on the froth of her coffee to cool it. And the sunlight gave her friend's face an alluring glow. 'Well, that gig brought *you* good fortune, didn't it, Fiona?' Deirdre said.

Fiona's mind spun through the years, to the time she'd started writing – without telling anyone. Now it was comforting recalling a particular passage she'd written, set on a train from Belfast to Dublin.

Crossing the Broadmeadow Estuary, the ebb tide was flooding through a gap in the causeway.

'It's like the water's boiling,' I said. 'Look at the strength of it.'

They turned to catch a glimpse of the swirling mass of ocean. '"There is a tide in the affairs of men. Which, taken at the flood, leads on to fortune." Isn't that Brutus in Julius Caesar?' he said.

Straining to keep sight of the water, I finished the line. '"Omitted, all the voyage of their life is bound in shallows and in miseries."'

I looked out to sea, not wanting to think about love failing, only about happiness.

Now, a windowpane rattled in the wind. The television flickered in the corner, mute. A garda car had called to the house earlier. Con was about to officially become a missing person. Had she driven a sick man from his home? Her earlier rage had now turned into worry.

Nóra, their 21-year-old daughter, came into the room, rubbing her arms and looking absently around her, a coat and scarf on.

'I have a project to do, but I just can't concentrate, Mam.'

'Where are you off to?'

'I'm so worried about Dad. I just feel like doing *something*. I'm going out to look for him.'

4

Con stares at the river. He wants to touch the surface, to feel the texture. Its constancy and certainty always brought him solace, but now it's puzzling him. Where do all those ripples go?

A whirring noise comes from behind. He ducks as a fishing line floats over his head, the spinner landing with a plop. Two boys stare at the lonely-looking man. 'Mister, mister, you're in our way!'

He's tired. Last night's hostel was a restless place; the bed was fine, but men were shouting, looking for drink, scrapping, having nightmares. He couldn't remember the last time he'd slept in a dormitory.

The woman behind the counter in the café looks familiar. He scratches his stubbled face trying to remember as he orders.

'An Americano, please?'

'Yes,' she says, starting to work the hissy machine.

He was sitting with the coffee when she came over to clean the table. 'Con Twomey, is it?'

He stares at her.

'Do you not remember me? Kate!'

She was an old flame, a relationship from the 80s. The years had brought furrows, but he remembered how amazing he used to think she looked. He wasn't so sure now. *Maybe she feels the same?*

'So, what's been happening in your life?' he asks.

'That's a long story,' she says as she wipes.

'How's your …?' Con asks.

'Oh, that ended a long time ago.'

Things had gone belly-up, she told him. Her marriage and nice house were gone. She was living in a small flat.

'Wasn't your husband a chemist?'

'Yes,' she says, looking away into the distance, still holding the cloth.

'So … he went off *experimenting* with someone else?' Con says with a wheezy chuckle.

'Glad I'm not looking for sympathy from *you*,' she says.

'Sorry … I didn't mean to …'

She returns to the counter. Con finishes his coffee and makes for the door.

A voice comes from somewhere. 'Good afternoon. What can we do for you?' It's later in the day and he's wandered into the city library. Sitting down with a scrapbook in front of him, he thumbs through cuttings and photographs of the great days of Rory Gallagher. He wants to be back there, in the ecstatic crowd, the guitar hero singing out across the prairie – about cowboys, and Buffalo Bill – the prairie of Cork City Hall that is.

He thinks about Fiona. She's fighting with Rory for space in his head. Fleeting scenes from the night they met, his enraptured walk back to the apartment that night, her phone number on a piece of paper in his pocket.

Yet he doesn't think of a family – his family – frantic now with worry. He's back to the day he met her parents, Fiona collecting him in her father's new BMW. They started with a spin to the beach at Dollymount, walking to where gentle waves came over the sand. A couple of ships lay motionless, waiting to get into the port; the city was hazy and still, except for sun glinting off windows on one or two high buildings. Beyond, the Wicklow mountains rose, their forests, heather, and rocky terrain just one blue haze.

'The tide's coming in,' he said, staring out to sea. 'The most powerful force on earth, you know?'

The sea was silently inching up the sand, foam bubbles breaking. Fiona dashed back to the car, threw it into reverse and used the accelerator a bit too enthusiastically, so the machine roared as it jolted to firmer ground. Following on foot, Con laughed at how scared she was. He saw her bless herself as the engine returned to its mannered hum. That was a thing his mother did.

At Howth Summit, they were convinced they could see the mountains in Wales. He pictured the bright heather, the Irish Sea shimmering, somebody trying to fly a kite, hikers passing, a hare darting. He touched her face. They kissed. He remembered the certainty of her lips that day. As he held her, he caught sight of a yacht out in the bay and was sure he could hear the wind flapping its canvas sails. It was that kind of day.

Soon they were on a leafy road and pulling into a well-maintained driveway. Affluent, he thought, standing in the hallway, a space big enough for a serious-looking antique table. In a reception room, a Bösendorfer grand piano had pride of place. On it was a framed family photo that must have been taken when Fiona was in her early twenties. She was wearing a loose-fitting top and leggings and looked more rounded than now. He thought he sensed tension of some kind in the faces.

Fiona's parents appeared. 'I'm Brendan,' said the grey-haired man. 'This is Jean.' A glamorous-looking woman shook his hand. He saw the delicate features she shared with her daughter. She clearly took care of herself and wasn't short of confidence when she spoke. Con could see the family building business had financed creature comforts, though a heart condition meant Brendan had taken a back seat recently.

Fiona's mother served dinner on delicate china, ethereal birds swooping around its edges. Brendan went on about a Burgundy terroir as he poured wine, as if he knew the actual vines and soil intimately. Wine was rare in Con's home, except at Christmas; drinking was something you did in a pub.

'Tell us about your family, Con?' Brendan asked.

Con decided to be provocative. 'My father had a distinguished career on the Cork docks. He's a Professor Emeritus of cargo handling, you could say. My mother has great skill with a mop and duster.'

Fiona had told him that her parents could be snobby, so he was being mischievous.

'I see,' said her dad. 'But you made it to university, didn't you?'

Con and Fiona shared a nervous smile. Her dad couldn't resist goading. 'I found it so hard to get fellas to do a good day's work for me.'

Con thought of his father, sweating in the hold of some ship or other. 'Is that right? Maybe Dubliners just don't have what it takes?' he ventured.

Jean, a Limerick native, nearly choked on her wine. 'Up Munster!' she said, to lighten things. They left it at that, moved to the sitting room, where Brendan opened a bottle of port. How Victorian, Con thought.

At the piano, Jean did a passable rendition of Thomas Moore's 'Believe Me, If All Those Endearing Young Charms', adding to the period feel of the evening, her fingers dainty and deft on the keys.

'What about a song, Con?' said Brendan.

Both men were a little tipsy.

Con stood up. 'You'll be expecting a Cork song, but I'll try a Dublin one, from James Joyce.'

He began with a flourish:

Have you heard of one Humpty Dumpty ...

'Ha,' said Brendan, interrupting him. 'I haven't heard that one for a long time.'

Con skipped to the third verse, to sing with relish:

He was father of all schemes for to bother us
Slow coaches and immaculate contraceptives for the populace

Looking at her daughter, Jean laughed politely. All three were glad to applaud when Con's memory ran out of verses.

'Do you know, I'll have to find myself a bus,' he said. 'Thank you for a lovely evening.'

Fiona walked him to the bus stop. He didn't notice her parents at the window, watching their daughter protectively.

'Excuse me,' a voice says. 'I'm sorry but you have to leave now. The library is closing.'

'Oh.'

Walking again, east this time, along Union Quay, then past the elegant grey edifice of City Hall, to where the river starts to widen, he passes the site of The Lobby Bar. Music once cast a magic spell on him there. The junction of Kennedy Quay and Victoria Road rang a bell; his father, Willie, was part of a dwindling breed of men who'd laboured here on the Cork docks, a man with big industrial hands, rough from blisters, enlarged over the years by labour. Working in gangs, the men shovelled anything from coal to slag, potash, and even milk powder. Camaraderie got them through the toiling. Some even brought their family dogs to catch rats hiding in the cargo.

Urinating on their hands to prevent blisters was normal. This tightly knit world had its own legends, men with nicknames like 'Top of the Egg', 'Lovely Knickers' and 'Ate the Fish'. He remembers a ballad he'd heard about such men:

Their lungs filled with coal dust
With their shirts stuck to their backs
And the arms that raised their glasses
Had raised a million sacks.

There was drinking in the city's early houses. Con's father struggled with the demons of pints and small ones in the dark corners of bars. He eventually won. He had other interests. *Wasn't it he that got me into Dylan?*

The incoming tide has stemmed the river's flow once again. Mist swirls in silently from the east. He watches a solitary man staring out to sea from a ship's deck, and wonders where the hulk might be bound for, what kind of a life it is for someone? A gull swoops above his head, a witness to his thoughts; that mass of water wasn't an innocent thing at all. It could do a lot of damage, that river.

5

Fiona sat examining her swollen ankles, sore from hours of scouring back laneways, navigating abandoned consumer goods among the weeds – in Turners Cross, Shandon, the Mardyke – looking for what, she wasn't sure: a wandering man, her damaged husband, discarded clothes, a body? Could another piece of waste ground or derelict doorway produce anything, except curious faces noticing her anguished look?

Because of the Alzheimer's diagnosis, Con was categorised as a high-risk missing person. Ending up in the river couldn't be ruled out, so both the Lee and Cork Harbour were surveyed. There were the inevitable false leads: a police car called to the house one evening with a jacket that had been found. Fiona looked at the garment, limp in the garda's hand and wondered what sad story it might reveal, a lost soul somewhere, before shaking her head. It wasn't Con's.

She was consumed with rumination, constantly looking to the past for clues – a seed of something untoward starting to take hold in her husband's head.

A drama was playing on the radio, *The Plough and the Stars*, a favourite of his. The Dublin tenement house sounded so real, filled with humour and humanity in the middle of crisis, a hundred years earlier.

Dozing off, something brought her back to student days, to the afternoon in 1984 when James showed her around his family's big house in Dartry, overlooking a beautiful park.

'It's tranquil here,' she said, looking out at mature trees producing another springtime of fresh growth. Ducks squabbled in a pond; a happy-looking couple were posing for wedding photos under a giant Scots pine. She heard a guitar behind her; James was sitting on the edge of his bed, a bottleneck skimming the frets – atmospherically, she thought.

'*This* is my thing,' he said, as if studying literature wasn't.

His music was seducing her as much as anything else about him, though she still hadn't decided if he was a dilettante, or someone she wanted to get closer to. She rocked back and forward as he played, quirked an eyebrow and smiled, drawn into this world of strings vibrating, a voice howling – about lonely people waiting for trains, lamenting their lot in cotton fields, or thinking they were cursed. Posters of Black men with guitars lined the walls. But in pride of place, a big map of the American South marked with circles and arrows. A loud strum ended the song and James said, 'That's where I want to go.'

A couple of weeks later, the guitar lay unplayed as things got passionate. The bluesmens' lived-in faces could only look down from the walls as shoes, jeans and underwear came off as things got hot; the levee shimmered, though a March wind was rattling the windowpanes in Dublin, accompanying a whirlwind of romance and sex. Afterwards, the inexperienced Fiona wondered why the sex, though pleasurable, had to be rough like this. But falling in love had dismissed any worries. James had mystique; he was good-looking, confident, funny. His attentions made her feel good. In the intervening years, she often wondered was it the macho side of him that she fell for. Was she an innocent?

When exams were over and the time came to make the travel arrangements to work in New York, followed by an adventure in the Southern states, they stood hand-in-hand in the queue outside the US embassy. They might find work, but the reality was that, with their families' resources, they didn't really need to.

'You're going *where?*' her parents said in unison. 'On your own?'

The answer brought them only partial relief. 'With James, I think I mentioned him, from my year, he lives in Dartry. And I'm 21, you know.'

Her dad's stony expression, her mother swallowing hard, with eyes half closed, made Fiona feel heartless. But Fiona couldn't resist the pull she felt towards James – then.

June 1984. The bell went on the last exam paper, she put down her pen and let out a huge breath in the hall. A week later she and James were on a plane across the Atlantic. They were disorientated when they arrived – America was noisy, the buildings big, the people loud, constantly leaning on car horns it seemed; coffee was served in buckets, not cups, the food proclaimed quantity rather than quality, there was heat and dust and grubby streets everywhere, she kept hearing calls of, 'Hey, lady!' wherever she went. But it was America, still so alluring.

They took hotel jobs for a few weeks, then took Greyhound buses south and west, ending up in Clarksdale, Mississippi. James's great wish was to stand at the crossroads near the city where legend had it that the great bluesman Robert Johnson had met the devil (she recognised the man with the hat and the guitar from the poster in James's bedroom), who took Johnson's guitar, infused it with power and offered it back to him, in return for his soul – so the tale from 1938 went.

James was disappointed there were no atmospheric, dusty roads meeting in the fabled countryside. The supposed setting of the Johnson story, the junction of highways 49 and 61, was now a nondescript suburb, the lore evaporated by urban sprawl. Not a sign of a bluesman or woman. But there was at least a nod to the legend – a crossroads-themed sculpture made with intersecting guitar necks. James stood in the middle of the road for a photo and nearly got run over by a pickup truck, driven by a yelling, bearded man.

The map again. Fiona wanted to try to find the legendary Tallahatchie Bridge, the one that Billy Joe MacAllister had jumped off in the Bobby Gentry song.

'But that's an hour or two away,' said James, slapping the map, 'for a … *pop* song!'

Disagreements were getting more frequent – the relationship unravelling; someone who seemed so alluring in Dublin had fallen to earth as a petulant brat – and worse. He'd turned intimacy into something ugly.

'James, it's a song of mystery and understatement, do you not get that?'

He couldn't see that it mattered to her, or just didn't care.

But why was this all coming back now? Con was her priority. And there was a task she wasn't looking forward to; she'd been advised to check for clues to his whereabouts among his things, to go through pockets, for starters. When she opened his laptop and watched it come to life, it felt like invasion of privacy, but there might be leads on it, she knew.

The machine wanted a password. She tried her own name, forwards and backwards, then Con's date of birth. Then she tried the children's names one by one. When she combined the two, the icons started to appear with an approving sound. It felt like she was entering a world she'd never been in before, rather than just snooping.

There were lots of files to look at, copies of contracts, bits of programme ideas, an attempt at a short story, even.

She couldn't resist opening the pictures: the family on boats, on beaches, everyone younger and looking happy. Fiona and Con windblown at the Cliffs of Moher, she wet with sea spray on a ferry, looking like she'd never have a care in the world.

Her heart skipped a beat when she saw a strange woman smiling at the camera, with a statue and the sea in the background. She looked closer, thinking Copenhagen's famous mermaid was gazing knowingly at the couple. 'What the ...' she murmured, getting more worked up at the static image, her imagination on overdrive – mermaid, myth, cool Scandinavia. *Bastard! He didn't take me there!*

Closing the folder, an ironic urge came, to assert, to repossess romantic times from their past, strolling through Dublin holding hands, drinking pints, walking the echoey floors of the National Gallery. In her imagination, she heard the drone of the 15 bus as it carried her, excited, towards Rathmines one day. The driver got a green light at the Grand Canal and the bus sailed over the reedy waterway. Pearse Hutchinson's poem came to mind:

When on the crest of the bridge at Portobello
the double-decker bus paused, for a minute,
and you – child, boy, youth, young man –
sitting in the front seat left on the top deck
had all Rathmines spread out before you
the sweep of the road as the bus swooped down again
your whole being through your eyes feasting
now rapturous now serene

She blessed herself (it was automatic) as the bus hurtled past the Church of Mary Immaculate. *Mary Immaculate* – how ironic, she a hypocrite, on her way to a tryst, to sex outside marriage? Fiona wasn't immaculate; she'd had sex before – in that difficult time she wanted to forget. And as for faith, she'd found it then, had journeyed from agnostic to believer; it had helped her through that James time and the aftermath.

Tonight, her heart, body and conscience were in a three-way argument. The Church couldn't be right about everything. She was 32 years of age and still single and she'd heard the sermons about the importance of family. Didn't God want people to fall in love, be happy? She thought of Mary portrayed with that sympathetic face. Didn't *she* believe in love?

Don't lose this man, her inner self said.

There'd been a false start the year before, a tentative romance with a teacher colleague, in the girls' school she'd taught in since she qualified as a teacher in 1986. As time went by, Fiona still believed romance was bubbling – a misreading of the situation: the engaging chats shrank to, 'Oh, hi, Fiona.' One day he arrived at the staffroom, beaming, and announced his engagement. Ashen-faced, she left the room – mortified her feelings might be revealed. Classes that morning seemed unusually long, the kids noisy, unwilling to learn.

Now, everything looked brighter. She pressed the STOP bell, feeling a tingle of nerves. Intimacy lay ahead.

'This is my little lair,' Con said, leading her into his flat. It looked fairly spick and span – he'd given it the once-over to impress her, she reckoned.

'Look at the view,' he continued, waving his hands. Through the window she could see a cricket ground, men in white were bowling and batting, the setting sun bathing them in orange light. The mannered sound of the ball being struck, and polite shouts, broke the air. 'It's straight out of PG Wodehouse, isn't it? They wouldn't last long on a hurling field,' he said, leading her to the little table where wine glasses waited.

Another anxiety came – bad memories she'd tried so hard to banish – sex as a coarse business. Now she just wanted a magic wand to summon ecstasy with someone she cared for.

The moment came; Con was sensual, yet she felt hesitant. At one stage she heard him ask if everything was OK. Touches of all kinds then worked their magic. Self-consciousness about features of her body was forgotten. She felt confident enough as the minutes elapsed to decide that there was no such thing in sex as being out of practice, it's the moment that matters; passion's resources can be summoned by the brain. Yes – everything *was* OK. At a crucial moment, as their bodies convulsed, she heard a cheer from the cricket field.

As they lay on the bed afterwards, Con spoke softly: 'You like Dylan, don't you?' Con asked, as he held her close.

'You mean like, "Lay, Lady, Lay"? she laughed. 'Well, I just did!'

He rubbed her leg, approvingly.

'Of course, I like Dylan,' she said, smiling. 'I love that one, "Every Grain of Sand", where he's pondering existence and eternity, faith, those big questions.'

'At least in that one he was getting a little more subtle about his evangelism,' he said, shifting on the bed and deciding he'd tease. 'I prefer a song like … Jokerman.'

'Why is that?'

'Because you're not sure whether the Jokerman is the Devil, or Jesus Christ, maybe, or Bob himself!'

The chimes from the town hall clock sounded. Clothes were scrambled, nakedness covered, hair tidied.

'That was … nice,' she said.

Sex still felt like a guilty pleasure. She was conflicted. And Con's desire to arrange another afternoon of passion meant disclosing her plans for the coming weekend. 'I must tell you; I'm making a pilgrimage to Lough Derg next week. A bit of solitude.'

She couldn't tell him another reason: the comfort she'd found there in darker times.

'Interesting. I knew you were religious, but I didn't think you were *holy*. Fasting and praying for two days and nights is not something I fancy myself.'

It was a relief he wasn't totally dismissive. He moved closer – suggestively.

'Does anything else happen other than devotion?'

'Well, as a matter of fact …'

'Tell me more.'

'With all the penance and fasting, something kind of primeval can surface.' She described being in the church in the dead of night, practically hallucinating from lack of sleep, noticing a man she'd seen around the island, a couple of pews in front of her. There was something about him.

'He and I talked later, among the stations. Whispered, more like.'

'You're a holy flirt!'

'It was a chaste chat,' she said, pleased at the alliteration. 'About the rain expected later; the challenge of it all, with a little eye contact born out of … accord.'

He put his arms around her, a tender gesture she appreciated.

She described the processions, the bells, murmuring pilgrims, the sound of hymns, the smell of wax, the patter of rain on plastic capes, damp bodies, the silence of prayer, darkness, candles, *Hail Mary, full of grace* … the solidarity of faith. Somehow it brought them closer. On the island she knew she'd say special prayers. Would she decide to tell Con about things from her past? No; it might spoil things. It would do some other time.

All the years later, she regretted it, sitting with a mug of tea, a drink that made her contemplative, the hot liquid reminding her of how much the Con she knew liked the comforts of home, the ones he'd forsaken. Fretting, she thought of all the places he might be. Maybe he'd left Cork and was living it up somewhere? Had he sneaked away to be with *her*?

6

A lonesome frontier between yesterday and today, Nóra thought, lying awake, listening to the swelling dawn chorus, trying to identify the bird songs echoing around the neighbourhood. What were they saying? Was it territorial, were they searching for a mate, or was it loneliness, even?

Her dad had been missing for three days. She got up, pulled on clothes, made tea, and set off to walk around the southside of Cork. Maybe it was just chasing shadows, but it was proactive, at least.

The front door click behind her was loud, the familiar street like somewhere unknown. A noisy van, dropping a bundle of newspapers to a dark shopfront, was the first sign of life. Walking towards the city, a lonely-looking man stared, and she stared back, imagining it was her dad. Lack of sleep was playing tricks on her.

The same father could annoy her sometimes with his old jokes, constantly repeating his good advice. Or, he'd hug her and say, 'Nóra Twomey, I'm so lucky to have you for a daughter.'

But the hug got weaker, and bonier, his body shrinking almost by the week. The lively father was still there, but struggling. They watched him stare at his pint, and lose interest in gigs, like the ones he would drag them to from time to time – old fellas, big bellied behind their guitars, playing endless solos, as if stuck in some groove from long before she was born.

She bit her nails as she walked. They were wrecked at this stage, but she didn't care; calamity had come to her family, neighbours asking questions, one or two a bit disingenuous, as if they were looking for scandal. She was trying to get on with her nursing course.

Her mother kept saying she didn't know why he might have left the house that day. 'Hasn't the disease made him more dependent on us?'

'Yes, Mam, but …' She thought there was something her mother wasn't telling her about – a row, maybe.

One night, a racy plot in a TV serial made her wonder would he have gone to meet a woman in another country? Her mother was on a different tack. 'What happened to folksy serials?' she wondered, as the credits rolled. 'In the old days there'd be all kinds of crises, but everyone seemed to end up all jolly in the pub. Where did all the darkness come from?'

'Morning, love,' a voice said. A man looked at her curiously – lecherously, she thought. She pulled up her hood and quickened her pace. A car went by with the windows down, blasting something that sounded like trance music, as if trying single-handedly to wake the whole city.

She looked at the pavement ahead of her and was soon in detective mode again: her dad had left his phone at home, so it couldn't be used to trace him; he had cash and his credit card, though by the time the hostel payment was discovered, he was gone. The Gardaí were sensitive about the possibility of him slipping deliberately into the river. She remembered his love of the Lee, how he observed the tides, sensed its moods almost. But no, he wouldn't do that. It didn't stop her nightmares about darkness and water and how long it would take to drown, and what if you changed your mind as the water surged around you?

The evening before, she saw her dad's guitar in the sitting room, picked it up, attempting the G major chord he'd shown her. The instrument twanged – with sadness. Would he ever play it again? The worry did strange things; nostalgia became vivid, her memory in overdrive. Nóra liked the present, but now found herself, for comfort, slipping back to a childhood world of reassuring images: her dolls, books with huge letters, jigsaws that never got finished.

Her parents moved about like shadows in her head, then splashes of colour, a smile, a hug, the aftermath of a row long forgotten. But the practical concerns would return, and the endless wondering. Other women in her dad's life? She didn't want to consider that aspect of her parents' lives; that they might find others attractive. It made her think about their relationship; in some ways, her folks were an odd match, her dad from working-class Cork and her mother a middle-class girl from a comfortable Dublin neighbourhood. How they met and fell in love was interesting – up to a point. They represented stability and security. And her dad slagging her mother about religion was part of that.

She knew that older people took comfort in faith. But she'd read enough about the horrible disease to know that kneeling in a church wasn't going to bring a cure. Was she missing something? Maybe comfort comes from a *belief* in intercession as much as actual intercession.

Nóra's teenage years were a time best forgotten; taking to the bed for days at a time, refusing to eat and refusing to speak to her worried parents. She'd hear a low hum of chat downstairs – most likely a discussion about her – but she couldn't help them understand, such were the low feelings that enveloped her. The world seemed to be ending; now she knew it was depression.

She and her dad became closer then. Somehow, his positivity about everything began to lift the gloom. A moment stood out, watching hot air balloons drifting dreamily over the Loire Valley, a blaze of colour above a field of rich, green vines. 'Those grapes could be crafted into a tasty drop of vino before too long,' he said, relishing the process that would transform them into wine.

Looking skywards, he meditated on Archimedes: that hot air being lighter than cold air allowed the balloon to rise when the air inside was heated. He had her staring at the sky as he did his amateur scientist thing. A nice memory now – of a different man. Crickets in the balmy air, as the balloons glided silently. 'How calming they are,' he said.

Nóra realised she'd come a long way from home. Around her, the day was in full swing. Commuters were beginning to settle in lines, in bumper-to-bumper traffic. A smell of coffee. A crowded bus. She began the trek home.

7

Máirín Toomey's hand shook as she poured a black, strong tea that Fiona didn't really care for, though she wouldn't dream of saying so. She loved Máirín, felt blessed to have her as a mother-in-law.

'No news feels like … bad news, doesn't it?' Máirín said, absently spooning more and more sugar into her cup, her eyes on a framed picture on the table – a smiling Con with a toddler Nóra on his shoulders, on a beach somewhere.

'You and Con are so happy together,' she continued, staring into space. 'And you really took to Cork, didn't you?'

'I did,' Fiona said, pouring milk liberally. Now she remembered that time, a summer's day in 1994, at Heuston Station. The word 'CORK' glowed from the departures board, along with a schedule of stops before the train would reach her new home. Two suitcases containing most of her life in Dublin rested at her feet. She'd applied for a teaching move – the difficult procedure involved joining a panel and waiting till a vacancy for her subjects, English and Irish, came up in a Cork school. She tried to relax her shoulders to look more confident than she felt. Her parents stood solemnly beside her.

'Mind yourself, won't you?' her mother fussed, mantra-like, as if she still hadn't accepted that their only child was leaving them.

The machine at the barrier examined and returned the one-way ticket; a whistle blast signalled her departure. The next episode of her life was on its way, a new house that she and Con managed to buy, with a sizeable contribution from her parents, in a new city.

They were moving because Con had developed an itch, feeling he was just a tiny cog in the TV schedule. Fiona was fond of telling him there were people who'd kill for his job. 'All that glamour?' she'd tease. But he couldn't help a growing disillusionment with life in a big organisation and made a leap of faith by setting up his own production company.

'Would you ever think about *not* living in Dublin?' Con had asked one evening, putting down his pint and tapping his fingers together on the hardwood bar of a pub he liked for its inner-city ambience, good pint, honest-to-God drinkers, men and women nursing their drinks with sporadic words and nodding heads.

'Well …' she began, then stopped, thinking of the certainty of her life in Dublin, her parents' neediness, the comfort of recognisable streets, the sun on Dublin Bay, Trinity College, where she might do a postgraduate course.

The train found its clacking rhythm, Fiona idly watching granite sheds and retired locomotives in rusty sidings. A woman laden with shopping bags took the seat opposite. 'My daughter is getting married next month,' she said proudly, manoeuvring her large frame into the seat. 'You have to have everything right.'

'Yes,' said Fiona, putting down her book and recalling her own hectic preparations only months before. There was no shortage of enthusiasm as she and the stranger discussed the joys, dilemmas, and perils of weddings. The secrecy of the dress, shoes, hair and make-up were discussed in detail. Ordering coffee when the trolley came around, only for Fiona's quick movement, her companion would have spilled it on the precious dress. 'Oh my God!' she said, hardly drawing breath and continuing her narrative.

As the train approached Portarlington, the woman gathered up her bags and Fiona was alone again. Unconsciously, she rubbed her wedding ring, thinking back to her own big day earlier that summer. She had wanted ivory for the dress, her mother had wanted white. 'Mum, all that stuff about virginity is taking tradition a bit far,' Fiona had protested. Her mother didn't argue but gave Fiona a knowing look. The discussion had an uncomfortable echo from the past.

Then it was about the jewellery. 'The jewellery has to be carefully balanced with the details on your dress,' Jean said. Fiona's friend, Emma, got involved too. She was planning her own big day at the time. 'What you wear on the day should be an extension of your personality,' she said. 'You're not a flashy person, Fiona, so you should tone it down on your wedding day. Less is definitely more.'

Fiona's dad, listening to the three of them talking, couldn't believe the detail and the supposed dilemmas involved – and couldn't resist throwing in his tuppence worth: 'Hannibal would have crossed the Alps and be on his way back by now.'

For Fiona, her wedding wasn't just a ring, a dress, a ceremony. There was a solemn side to it – marriage was a sacrament, one of seven, serving to express visibly what God is doing invisibly. The concept of grace appealed to her – a way to describe how God shares the divine life with us.

'Grace – it's a while since I heard that word,' Con said after she'd succeeded in bringing him to a pre-marriage course. Fiona felt that his buying in was an act of love in itself – he saw what it meant to her. On her way to meet him one evening, she'd stopped to visit the church on Rathmines Road, tiptoeing reverently through the large interior to the votive stand where candles flickered, setting the scene for her private reflection – on the past and future. The light in churches always affected Fiona; it sparked thoughts – epiphanies even. Now she watched the last sun of the day illuminating a stained-glass window, Mary at the Cross. The quest for happiness was uppermost on her mind, commitment to the rough and the smooth, to joy and pain. Marriage was a pledge, but not necessarily a misty paradise; relationships can flounder, people can change. Passion and contentment don't always go hand in hand, she reflected, watching Our Lady's glass image grow slowly darker.

On a warm Saturday in May, the old-world hotel close to a north Dublin beach made the day special. Thanks to the Cork contingent, all notions of a sedate affair went out the window. They brought partying to a new level: fearless renditions of songs, wild dancing, spilled pints, flirting. The families clicked, to Fiona's relief. Brendan got well-oiled, let it rip, taking to the pints with Con's uncles and some old colleagues of Con's dad. Their earthiness appealed to him, for the day at least. He even decided to play up his background, not something he did in his golf circle. Announcing he was Sheriff Street born and bred, he attempted a couple of verses of 'The Auld Triangle.' Fiona was mortified at his relish of Behan's lines about desiring the company of the female prisoners of Mountjoy.

Con was well on and began imitating Seán O'Casey's character, the Covey, in a mock Dublin accent. 'Comrade, did you ever read, Jenersky's *Thesis on the Origin, Development and Consolidation of the Evolutionary Idea of the Proletariat?*' He liked the misplaced idealism, and the dogged personality that made the man comic. Swaying, he continued the role-playing. 'Do ye mean to say … you *haven't* read it?'

Fiona saw Máirín give him a look to say he was getting a bit out of hand. They spoke softly to each other. He got the message and eased off.

'Why don't you give us a song, Mam?'

Máirín stood up straight away, coughed, swallowed, and waited till there was a hush around her. Out came her party piece, a cynical music-hall ditty, 'A Member of the Dáil,' delivered with panto-style hand gestures:

My brother he's a TD me boys, my brother he's a TD,
He got me mother the pension and she's only sixty-three …

She was a shy woman, yet she always liked the rare moments like this when the floor was hers.

Put up a grand new house for us and let the old one fall,
For it wasn't up to date enough for a member of the Dáil …

Fiona got tipsy herself and ended up going for a stroll on the beach with Con as night fell, allowing the expensive dress to trail across the soft sand. The moment was still vivid – the Irish Sea tranquil. Her husband looked so handsome in the moonlight, a man she hoped would give her certainty and memories to cherish. She leaned on his shoulder, wanting the day's happiness to stretch to the horizon.

The hooter woke her as the train entered the Blackpool tunnel, before descending into the city. At Kent Station, Con ran through the crowd to hug her. 'You're in the *real* capital now, Fiona!' he said.

She was so glad to see him after their couple of weeks apart – their life in Cork now concrete and real. The three-storey house that would be their home had character – she'd fallen for it at the first viewing. Fuchsia and foxgloves, attended by bees, covered the front garden.

Opening the door, a smell of fresh paint hit them; the bare floorboards in the hallway creaked invitingly. Fiona ran her hand slowly down the hardwood banister again. 'I'm going to be so happy here, Con.'

A man for important details, he'd sourced a nice antique bed with the money left over when all the house expenses were sorted.

'That's great,' she said, kicking off her shoes and trying the mattress.

'Direct from Oliver Plunkett Street,' he said, giving the frame a shake. He stopped talking to run his finger across the top of the skirting board and invited her to look at his finger with no dust on it. He'd bought a good vacuum cleaner and couldn't wait to start using it.

'I'm impressed,' she said.

Next day, taking a stroll to get a sense of the neighbourhood, they walked down Evergreen Road together. She tugged his arm. 'We have to see this church.' She'd heard about the world-renowned Church of Christ the King. Oddly shaped concrete towers and terracotta tiles appeared in front of them.

'Yes,' he said. He hadn't really appreciated the bold celebration of concrete. And he was distracted by a roar from Cork City's ground close by – a goal must have been scored by the home team.

The Art Deco triumph had been commissioned in 1927 and designed by a Chicago architect with a Cork-sounding name,

Barry Byrne, once a pupil of Frank Lloyd Wright. It was the nicest church she'd ever seen.

She dragged him to the entrance, adorned by an imposing figure of Christ, outstretched arms framing the doors. 'The body of Christ is a pillar, the arms are like trusses, supporting the church,' she said, suddenly becoming still. 'So *real*, isn't it?'

'I get what you mean,' he said, staring at the geometric shapes. 'The inside is supposed to be the engineering triumph,' he said, warming to her enthusiasm as they went inside. 'See, there are no pillars, no trusses. I don't know how they did it,' he said.

'A statement of belief by the architect,' she suggested.

She believed Con was starting to warm to her religious side. He'd seen how faith – the little rituals of prayer – had helped his mother so positively in her life. 'There's something appealing about the pageantry of Catholicism,' he said more than once.

'Well, come for the pageantry and you might stay for the message,' she would say.

She loved the feeling of power in communal worship, incense filling the church at Benediction, people joined together in belief – and hope. A choir could transport her, its spirit pressing pause on the material world.

In August, she took to lighting candles in St Augustine's church on Washington Street, conception on her mind. Above the entrance, a mosaic of a contented-looking Mary with baby Jesus was framed by the order's motto, '*Mater Boni Consilii*

Ora Pro Nobis' – Mother of Good Counsel, Pray for Us. Con told her that it was the church that Rory Gallagher used to attend with his mother when he still lived in the city.

'Maybe Rory will bring us luck?' he said.

'It might take more than that!'

During this time, she liked visiting Máirín, enjoying her gentle talk, the endearing way she shuffled about her kitchen making tea for them, sighing and reminiscing about the time called the 'old days'. She wouldn't ask direct questions about her and Con's family intentions but had a way of bringing up the subject. 'Next door just had their first grandchild. They're over the moon.'

One day she said gently to Fiona, 'Well, if it happens it'll be a gift from God.'

Fiona had another thought: was this fertility issue, this difficulty conceiving, God's way of judging her for something – a sin – in her past?

In December, after five months trying, the umpteenth testing kit produced the desired blue colour, bringing joy, but also feelings from the past she couldn't explain – or share with anyone.

In January, a teaching post came up in a girls' school nearby. Elation turned to nervousness. The first day was daunting: the girls' accents, their exuberance, their curiosity about what the new teacher, a Dubliner, might be made of. The teaching itself seemed to be the least of the challenges. 'I think I've lost it,' she said, arriving home bedraggled after the first day.

Con was reassuring. 'No, you haven't.'

A few weeks later, everything seemed settled. A pep in her step seemed to propel her the whole way to the school. One or two colleagues became friends. Lively staff-room discussions about the more colourful pupils could shorten the day. Her colleagues were a mixed bag: the dedicated and the devil-may-care, sloppy dressers and one man who was never without a tie. There were one or two union activists, and one mature colleague who did her job and was happy not to engage with anyone beyond the pleasantries. Fiona wondered what made her tick.

Phelim O'Sullivan, a man in his early forties, was a lively presence in the staffroom, and possessed an enviable ability to control noisy kids, but also an air of someone who didn't really want to be turning up dutifully at a school every morning. Fiona found that contrast with herself and her diligent way of doing things interesting. Once, a couple of colleagues nudged each other knowingly when she appeared in the staff room, and Phelim grew more animated. There was a kind of mutual admiration between them – nothing more in Fiona's case – but she always suspected that Phelim harboured romantic feelings for her. Then her bump appeared.

As her pregnancy progressed, she spent several weekends in Dublin. Her father was undergoing treatment for tumours in his lungs. After chemotherapy, the cancer there had been controlled, but it had spread, and was slowly and invisibly conquering his weakened body. 'My little girl ...' was all he could manage to say when he saw her at the end of the hospital bed. She knew he was happy for her; he liked Con.

She glanced guiltily at her watch – she needed to catch the last train back to Cork to see her gynaecologist next morning. Perhaps she and her father would never meet again – in this life at least. He fell asleep again, relieving her conscience. Yet the sound of his gentle breathing haunted her after she stepped away to leave. The hospital doors closing behind her seemed to make a callous sound, the taxi, the station, the platform, the whistles all made her want to feel the warmth of old times. Did she have to leave him? She couldn't believe how sad it felt – the strength of their bond. Would the next news be that he was gone? Would it be during her appointment the next day? Would she watch the baby's movements on a screen and cry out for her dad?

By September, the baby was in a breech position, so the birth was by Caesarean section. The day was a blur; she heard epidural mentioned, felt someone at her back and felt a needle moving inside her before all was calm. An occasional voice broke the silence. Machines beeped their reassuring accord, as if orchestrating the wonder of reproduction.

At the christening in Christ the King, the symbolism of the holy water falling on her little baby entranced Fiona, the priest naming him the third time the water touched the boy: Ciarán. His wail almost drowned out the priest's words. Fiona knew Con didn't share her views, but she was conscious of the obligation being bestowed on this tiny little being – according to the words of the ceremony, at least – to share in the Church's apostolic activity.

'He could end up a priest yet,' Con whispered as the ceremony concluded. 'That would please his mother!' He touched Fiona's arm. His joke belied the fact that he'd agreed that Ciarán would be raised a Catholic. He knew how much it meant to Fiona.

There was a party at the house. Everyone wanted to hold the baby. Fiona stood guard by the little wicker cot, a hand-me-down from Máirín. Amid the celebrations, a private moment came as she moved Ciarán to another room to let him sleep. The tiny infant's soft breathing brought thoughts of certain events a long time ago – physical trauma – that she wanted to banish on such a happy evening in her life.

The memories grew more vivid, and the clamour of the guests seemed to recede. Her feelings – a jumble of regret, guilt and pain – couldn't be shared with anyone. Another time, maybe. She tiptoed back to the party.

A phone rang, the ringtone set to 'Ode to Joy'.

'Is that yours?' Máirín shouted anxiously, nearly dropping her teacup.

Fiona scrambled for her bag. It was Ciarán, breathless: a friend of his cycling through Lee Fields and had seen a man on a bench who, he said, 'looked the image of your da.'

'Are you going to have a look?' Máirín asked, hopping up from the chair, a sparkle in her eyes. Twenty minutes later,

Fiona and Ciarán were scouring the park in the twilight. No sign. They even examined the debris, cans and papers, for clues. They could see the Lee flowing on in the twilight. She thought of Con, raving about the surprise gig U2 had played here in August 1985. He could sing his way through their whole set. What she wouldn't give to have him doing that now. Poor Máirín, poor all of them; their glumness complete as another day ended.

Rowdy voices came from a group of lads drinking cans before one of them shouted, 'Hey! Any chance of a few coins?' The request seemed to add to their despondency.

8

Con and Kate sit with pints in the Shandon Arms.
'So, what's become of your life?' she asks. 'Weren't you in Dublin for a few years?'

'Yes.'

He'd arrived back at the café asking her to meet him for a drink (maybe he was fantasising about old times). He can hear bells ringing in the nearby Cathedral of St Mary and St Anne.

'I … I've been back in Cork a few years, and …' He stops talking.

'What's wrong?' Kate asks.

'Why did the bells just stop?'

'Bells do that,' she laughs.

They sip their pints.

'You have kids, don't you, Con?'

It triggers an odd reflection, from the time Fiona was trying to conceive – of sex as involuntary. 'It takes the fun out of sex,' he cackles.

'What?' She looks around in case anybody had heard him, before shifting the conversation. 'I bet you are a good father, though?'

He thinks about that, remembering his absorption in the details of milk and bottles, heating them in the middle of the night, when breastfeeding didn't work. Spontaneously he whispered lines from a lullaby about wind and haunted graves and angels watching over a child.

'What's that?' Kate asks.

He looks at her, but neither can remember the name of the Pogues song.

A lull in the conversation. Con leans closer to her. 'It's a fella called Phelim.'

'What do you mean?'

He whispers. 'I think she's had an affair with him.'

'Your wife, Con? Maybe you're imagining it,' she says sympathetically.

An hour passes, their glasses are empty, and Kate gets up from her stool. 'That was enjoyable, but I'd better head home.'

'I'll walk you there.'

He's not sure why he said this. As they ramble across the city, he grows increasingly flustered; what if she asks him in? He has visions of trysts from years before, long before he met Fiona, but they just disturb him.

He glances at Kate as she talks, her voice not as sensuous as it seemed way back then. When they get close to her road, she turns to him, 'Good to see you, Con,' smiles, and walks on. He watches her disappear, feeling relief more than disappointment.

He'll have one more pint, he decides, then he walks back to the quayside, close to the tall R&H Hall silos, where the two channels of the river re-join to flow onwards to Cork Harbour and the open sea. He stands for a while, enjoying the salty air, almost feeling the tide rise. The Idle Hour is beside him, an early house, with the spit-and-sawdust charm he likes in a pub. A faint cheer comes from inside, the excitement of a football match.

Ordering a pint, he looks indifferently as Barcelona and Lyon shirts dart across the screen, trying to remember what was it about football and this pub, once upon a time? Yes, it was when he and Fiona moved to Cork, and the night Ireland played Italy in the 1994 World Cup. Fiona joined him for the second half and Ireland were ahead. She asked him who had scored the crucial goal. Why did his memory go blank at that moment? He wonders now. The lads had laughed at him. 'Houghton, boi!'

Did it signpost things to come?

'Same again?' a voice says.

Con looks at the barman. 'No. It's OK.'

What is he doing here at all? All kinds of scenes flood his head. Nightmares about work, dreams where people he knew appear grotesque. Yet, it doesn't occur to him how worried Fiona and the kids might be by now. He knows home – that life – is somewhere close by but thinking of directions is confusing. Anyway, he can't face it. There's a dread inside him he can't really understand.

Outside, a murky darkness has descended. He feels like he's in a Claude Monet painting of London in the nineteenth century – everything hazy, mysterious, Thames bridges brooding, smoke billowing, light and fog merging, and diffusing. *Wouldn't it have been great if Monet had come to Cork? He could have immortalised the Lee.* He chuckles to himself.

Looking towards the river, he sees a ship's gangplank unattended. He can hear the deep hum of the engine. Where is it bound for? *Maybe I could hide somewhere and wake up in a beautiful place, spices in the air, exotic music playing, no troubles.*

He stares at it for a long time.

9

An afternoon in 2015, the Central Line train rattled and swayed, as if syncopating the beat of a Pogues song in Con's head. The combination eases his nerves. London seemed gigantic and forbidding; all those tube lines, escalators, passageways to negotiate, relentless advertising signs, wind blowing from the tunnels through crowds of endless faces, sparks flashing from receding trains, the constant electrical whiff.

He was on his way to a meeting in Soho. As he skipped up the steps from Oxford Circus station to walk the few hundred yards down Oxford Street, it was drizzling rain, a wind was blowing – just like in Shane McGowan's imagination. The song's evocation of a romantic encounter in a damp setting – someone falling into another's arms – gave Con a burst of expectation. Would this be *his* 'Rainy Night in Soho'?

They'd met a few weeks earlier in Cannes. The setting was the twice-yearly TV producers' gathering when he'd drifted into a lively-looking Scandinavian party on a terrace at one of the posh hotels on La Croisette. They got talking. He'd seen her before at one of these shindigs.

'I am Kirsten, from Denmark,' she'd said, sticking out her hand.

'I'm Con – from Cork,' he said.

'Where's that?' she asked, a glint in her eye.

As the night wore on, she enchanted him more and more.

An e-mail from her lit his inbox a few days later, a query about a programme idea they'd talked about, had him recalling her elegance, her mystery, as he replied, adding, 'I enjoyed meeting you.' E-mails back and forth continued. Con realised with a pang of guilt he'd told Fiona a lot about Cannes, described the mad Scandinavian party, the big talk from wannabe moguls, but hadn't mentioned the tall woman with the mischievous eyes and the laugh that made him feel carefree. When Kirsten said she'd be in London for a couple of days, a rendezvous was conspired. A crazy idea? What if she wasn't the person she'd seemed? He knew he'd have to make up a story about going to London to Fiona – loving, caring, innocent of planned infidelity.

Now, close to the rendezvous place, a woman stood looking in his direction. He passed her before realising who it was and turning to see her face glowing from a streetlamp.

'You walked past me!' she said.

She was as willowy as he remembered, and the wind caught her shoulder-length hair as she smiled at him.

'Kirsten?'

'Yes, of course.'

The cat missing, the car giving trouble, the kids' exams, a water leak that needed fixing – all flashed by – fading quickly. This was exciting.

'Will we go for a drink?' he asked, saying the words like twenty years of marriage were suspended – happy to lose a brief argument with his conscience.

'Would you like a short history of me?' he asked, handing her a dry white wine. She heard his account of his childhood in a frugal neighbourhood in Cork, his television ups and downs. 'I think I'm not a bad dad, I'm an OK husband. But here I am on this … *date*.'

'Don't analyse too much,' she smiled.

She was married with one son. Equality of infidelity, he thought. Yet she avoided explaining why she was here. 'I just found you interesting and wanted to see you again. So …'

It sounded like both a punctuation and question.

The pub noise dipped as he spontaneously bent over and kissed her.

'Would you like to join me in my room? The mini bar is well stocked,' she asked when he walked her back to her hotel.

The fizz of tonic on gin never sounded so promising. It wasn't particularly hot, but she took off her jumper. He was self-conscious about his hands – had to do something with them. He touched her bare shoulder and felt the texture of her skin. They kissed again. Approving murmurs suggested a point of no return. Something clicked. They were on the bed, clothes discarded – awkwardly by him, dextrously by her.

Primitive skill took over, the real world paused, in a series of small events – touches, requests, directions, amendments, approvals, whispers, sighs – modesty forgotten as they improvised scenes from their own erotic drama. He heard ecstasy expressed in a foreign language.

He might have heard rain, a refuse truck beeping its way down the street, but it didn't distract from the intimacy. He thought about the size of London and wondered how many other people were having sex with people they weren't supposed to be with at that moment. Was it going as well for them?

Thunder woke him later, a flash of lightning illuminating brocade wallpaper. He was in a song again, U2's 'Electrical Storm,' the sound of the band vivid, Bono singing about lovers on a bed as day breaks during a storm. Right enough, dawn had come.

A couple of hours later, tired but high, he watched the clicking destination board at cavernous Paddington station. 'I think that's my train' she said, pointing at the whirring place-names. He even liked the way she waved her hand. Looking at him intently, she closed her eyes, waiting for his lips.

'Let's meet again?' she said, turning to go.

'Yes …'

He watched her train disappear into the morning.

A few hours later, as the taxi from Cork Airport navigated the southside of the city, he was rehearsing the stories he'd have to make up as reality kicked in and the driver griped about football and politics as the all-too-familiar roads around Turner's Cross came into view.

Fiona was in great form; a satisfying enough day at the school, she reported.

'How are Nóra and Ciarán?' he asked.

'Nóra's such a little innocent, in her own world. I saw her with that dreamy look as she did her homework.'

Had he been betraying this harmony, responsibility, in London? He changed the subject. 'How did your book club go?'

'Oh, yes. It was short stories by an English writer, Tessa Hadley. Characters have curious reflections – epiphanies, you could call them – after sex.'

'Interesting,' he said nervously.

'She writes about … the emotional effects of sensual activity, the price we can pay for pleasure.'

'It must have been an interesting discussion?'

She laughed. 'Well, as a matter of fact, one of us – I won't say who – started getting a little … confessional.'

'Really?'

'She said some very raw things about her marriage and wondered to the group what had happened to passion in her life.'

'That's fairly out there.'

He left it at that and offered to make tea, but Fiona continued. 'Maybe it was the wine, but she told us about an affair that didn't work out. We were all ears, till she burst into tears. The guilt really got to her.'

Guilt? He became suddenly intrigued by the workings of the kettle. But his mind was churning, contrasting stability and contentment with passion and adventure; between this woman he cared so much about, and the bewitching powers of a stranger, whose touch he could still almost feel on his body.

———————————

Weren't the Buddhists right, Fiona thought as she lay wide awake later that night; consequences follow actions. Infidelity doesn't just happen; it's a choice people make. Choices eventually catch up with you. But what she'd told Con was only part of what had happened at the book club – a sanitised version of events. There were things she'd never told Con, despite all their years together. Was she guilty of dishonesty? No. Wasn't it just some of the mystery every person was entitled to?

Neither had she shared her thoughts with the other women. Talk about affairs, sex, attraction was fine, but the subject cut too deeply for Fiona, who mostly listened in silence, surprised by how disturbed it made her feel.

The walk home was reflective: what is it about human beings that attract them to others? Why can things get so deep between people, then fall apart suddenly? Is attraction that fickle? She remembered how unhappy she was at one stage in her life, the way something turned so sour; what began with infatuation, passion, magic, turned into awkwardness, recoil, distaste. It was all so quick. She shuddered, and not from the cold wind that blew around her that night.

Con made a noise beside her, mumbled something and she looked at him. Isn't there only so much you know about another person, what goes on in their mind, or their heart, even though you might sleep in the same bed with them for years? So close, yet maybe so far away.

There wasn't a sound from the street. She thought of the silence of the body itself, the soundless processes of the brain; all that complexity worked away in quietness. Hearts beat, but their deeper functions – those that make-or-break human beings – are silent. Things go right and things go wrong in there. And emotions can be made to rise to storm force. And the people who can cause this tumult in us, we only met by chance or luck.

Go to sleep, she told herself.

10

The morning after his London trip, Con stood leaning against the parapet of Christy Ring Bridge, watching the river. It had potency – strength and certainty – as it flowed from the west, swollen by tributaries whose names he knew by heart: the Sullane, Foherish, Laney, Dripsey, Bride, Glasheen. The waters arrived at the city carrying legend and lore. *There might be a series there?* Daydreaming done, he continued towards his office.

A nameplate on the door announced Shandon Screen, the production company he'd set up with a pal, Pat Roche. Taking the stairs two at a time, he passed a picture of himself having a serious-looking discussion with a celebrity. Inside, the four office desks hosted computers and mountains of untidy paperwork; a dusty bookshelf bowed under the weight of music histories, guidebooks, and biographies. Described as a suite, the second room contained cameras, lighting gear, chargers, and anything that could conceivably be useful in the future.

Pat brought family money and a good business sense to the partnership. Con's return to Cork made perfect sense to him. Dublin was 160 miles up the road, but a whole world away; it didn't matter that its media scene dwarfed Cork's. 'Aren't you delighted you're back in the beautiful city, Con?' he'd often say.

Con rubbed his hands. Pitching for work could be a nail-biting affair – the lows of rejection, the highs of a commission. Now an e-mail confirmed another series of *Sounds of Summer*. He'd spend a few weeks travelling around Ireland again, filming musicians on the fringes of festivals, a couple of visiting big names too. Shot and edited on a shoestring, the broadcaster would play the six programmes against a drama serial, so not too much was expected in terms of audience share. He imagined his cast of musicians and singers were delighted to get the chance to perform on a TV stage.

The tryst with Kirsten was distracting him too. What was he doing in London? Wasn't he being a complete rat? His and Fiona's lives were intertwined: home, children, family. The liaison threated to disrupt everything. Was it a fleeting thing, or might it lead somewhere else?

A text came: 'Back to work today but feeling happily unsettled – x'

He heard the stairs creak, the office door opened and in walked Pat. 'Howya, boi,' he said. He fancied being a Cork city character, but he was a middle-class kid. 'Bet ye had it hot and heavy with some fancy wan away in London?'

Con blushed. 'We have the summer series!' he said, to change the subject.

'Great stuff,' said Pat. 'It might be worth a pint later?'

Con considered himself the punctual, serious one; Pat could roll in late, then come up with a great idea or useful business insight. He was one of those people with a strategic mind. They could annoy each other, but the partnership worked.

Coming up with a hit format was the gold standard for independent companies at that time. Shandon Screen's latest attempt was called *Meet Your Memories*. They liked the paradox of the title. Studio-based, songs would trigger happy, embarrassing, or tragic memories for participants. They'd be surprised on the set by someone from their past, triggering emotion (they hoped) about a forgotten moment in their lives. But the idea still needed a twist. This morning was set aside for another brainstorm session.

Con noticed Pat staring at him a couple of times. 'It's not like you to have so many unopened emails?'

The remark felt like an intrusion as Pat stood over his shoulder staring at Con's screen.

'Let's crack into this?' Con said, a flip chart and marker in hand. They weren't flip chart people. But they tried, at least.

'Who the feck thought up dis stuff?' Pat said. '"Threats" and "Opportunities" how are ye! There's a great opportunity – for a pint!'

By four o clock, brainstorming done, they were restless and thinking about a drink. They headed to a pub they both liked, The Old Reliable, an insalubrious but friendly house. The regulars found Con and Pat a kind of curious novelty.

'Hey, men, how are ye?' said the barman.

'We'll have a Murphy's and a Beamish,' said Con.

One of the regulars was reading the sports page of the *Echo*. He and Pat supported Liverpool; Con, Man United. Talk started about the two teams clashing the previous weekend. Suddenly, Con started singing.

In your Liverpool slums
you look in the dustbin for something to eat …

Everyone looked at him, Pat frowned, but Con continued.

… you find a dead rat and you think it's a treat …

'Feck off, ya langer!' Pat said, with a frown, trying to diffuse the discomfort; there'd been no reason to burst into song. Con hadn't read the mood of the company.

The barman smiled as he dragged a cloth over and back across the counter as the chat continued, about hurling now; how were Cork going to do in the championship?

Con reached for his phone; a text had come from Fiona. He'd almost forgotten their arrangement to meet in a restaurant on The Mall, at six, for a family dinner. There were a couple of other messages too – one from foreign parts.

'I'm off, Pat.'

'Fair enough. I'll stay for one more,' he said, signalling to the barman. 'We'll have loads of brainwaves by next week, boi.'

Passing Shandon church, Con saw it was six o'clock already. Checking texts as he walked, he saw one from Kirsten. 'How has your Friday been? I'm missing you. It would be nice to see you again x.' But there was also that niggling voice, his guilty conscience. *What was I thinking, sneaking away like that? Would he do it again?*

Crossing the road to take steps down to Devonshire Street, he felt something happen with his balance. Seconds later, he was face down on the ground. He must have lain there for a few seconds because he began to feel the cold of the street on his chest. He pulled himself up, disorientated. The bump on his forehead was stinging and tender.

'What happened you? asked Fiona when he joined them in the restaurant.

'I just slipped,' he said. 'It's frosty out there.'

'You look a bit of a mess. Were you and Pat at the pints again?'

'Just two, as it happens.'

She described her afternoon with a class at the Crawford Gallery, loving the ambience of the early-eighteenth-century building.

'It was going well till the sculpture section presented a good opportunity to try and embarrass me,' she said wearily. 'When we got to the cast of Boëthus's 'Boy and Goose' sculpture, of a naked cherub grabbing the bird by the throat, hilarity broke out; "'Miss, it's very small!" – that kind of thing. But I managed to get things back on track,' she said confidently.

Next stop was a painting of Donegal schoolchildren by Muriel Brandt. What were the children in this painting thinking about, Fiona had asked the girls, were they happy, or sad, or maybe bored?

'The idea of ambiguity in the human gaze silenced them. It was something from my afternoon of crowd control,' she said. And –'

Con put down his glass suddenly, interrupting her with a puzzled expression. 'Don't they have that painting there, "The Fall of the House of Usher",' He was referring to a dark work by Harry Clarke, the painter articulating grotesque imagery in the style of Edgar Allen Poe.

'There's something about it I don't like,' said Con emphatically. 'A person is entombed, but still living. It's creepy, like your worst nightmare … a grim idea for a painting. It freaks me out. I don't want to ever see it again,' he said very deliberately.

Ciarán looked at him and tried to make light of the outburst. 'Dad, it's only a *painting*.'

As they walked home later, Con stopped abruptly. 'Sorry, but I suddenly got this strange feeling about that painting. It seemed to be alive and threatening me. I can't explain how it makes me feel.'

He fell silent for the rest of the journey. The others kept stopping, trying to identify stars. He felt indifferent to the heavens. A feeling that something might be going wrong came over him. What was it?

11

Nóra not only walked the streets, paced the floor, pondered the past looking for clues, she also made notes – like a detective. *Tonight, I said to Mam casually, would Dad have gone to meet a woman in another country? She glared at me. It had just slipped out!*

The possible scenarios: he was somewhere else in Ireland; he was a stowaway and maybe across the equator by now; someone was sheltering him in Cork. But might it be something to do with her mother? She remembered once asking her granny Jean if her mam was as religious when she was younger. Jean gave her a you're-a-cheeky-kid glance and looked away into the distance. Was there something in her mother's life that had made her go back to faith? She also remembered a family holiday in West Cork when her Mam and Dad didn't seem to laugh with each other as much as they used to. Or maybe it was just the disease had begun?

One evening, she opened the family desktop computer – snooping, she admitted – and saw a file called 'Fiona stuff'. She paused for a few seconds, then opened it. She started reading – a scene set on a holiday:

I enjoyed the cool Atlantic spray hitting my face as we sailed to Clare Island from Roonagh pier. Con stood on the deck, pointing in different directions, trying to identify head-lands and islands. A trawler came across the bow, seagulls screeching at its wake, as if the birds were being towed reluc-tantly. He waltzed in time to the boat's sway, then sat down beside me.

'Do you remember the time we came here when the kids were small?'

'Yes.'

'Well, we were on the boat and there was this woman sitting close to us. She was wearing a delicate floral dress, crêpe de chine, perhaps. She was beautiful, too.'

'You've some memory.'

'Every time a gust of wind blew, it lifted the dress and she found it hard to control. Her upper legs were so shapely.'

'What?'

He started laughing. 'The kids were asking about Fungi the dolphin and I was telling them that that was in Dingle, at the other end of the country, and they were all disappointed.'

'And all their father was thinking about was some woman's legs.'

'Yes. It was something about them – and her. Then the breeze obliged once more as the boat rocked. It was so ... there's only one word for it, erotic.'

'Why are you telling me this?'

'I don't really know.'

I'd recovered from the burst of fantasy as we walked along a quiet road to St Brigid's Abbey, to see the island's ancient ceiling paintings. Inside, the light was low for conservation reasons, the dimness adding potency to the faded outlines of medieval art: hunting scenes, dragons, fishermen and figures playing primitive instruments, everyday life and mythological creatures represented side by side.

'Wouldn't this take your mind off the woman with the floral dress?' I said.

'What woman?'

'Never mind,' I laughed – briefly.

Nóra had to take a deep breath. Her mam must have written this since the diagnosis. She remembered a holiday trip to that same island way back when she was about seven or eight. Laughter, sun, sand, heat; a happy time.

Was it a memoir? Was there more? She scrolled to another piece:

A gloomy drive home from the clinic. The presenter on the car radio announced it was Willie Nelson's birthday. Up came the chugging harmonica and 'City of New Orleans', sparking other memories as I tapped on the steering wheel. I'd once taken the famous train out of Memphis, after touring Sun Studios, where the ghosts of Jerry Lee, Elvis Presley and Johnny Cash earned a crust for their enthusiastic guide. If only I could have enjoyed that time more?

In Greenwood we changed trains, to battered, creaking rolling stock that trundled past shotgun shacks and fallen brickwork, before rattling to an unscheduled stop among cotton fields. A turtle stared me in the eye from its patch. I imagined the creature saying, 'what are you doing here?'
— as if somehow, it sensed my turmoil.

Was all this imaginative, revealing — or just disturbing? Nóra went to bed unsettled, her mother appearing in a dream, now with a different — mysterious — aura.

12

'It's about fantasy,' Kirsten said.

Peacocks strutted around them, screams of fear and delight came from rollercoasters, colourful dancers made faces and waved fans. He was getting the Tivoli Gardens magic.

It was a balmy evening in May 2016, in Copenhagen. A mime show was in full swing near the terrace restaurant they chose for dinner. Kirsten studied the artists. 'You know, the interesting thing about mime is that it connects with the silence that's in us all.'

'Yes,' he said, trying to think of a rejoinder, impressed by the flow of her English. 'You put it very eloquently – as usual.'

They giggled.

She leaned towards him. 'It's good to see you again,' she whispered softly, before settling back in her chair and picking up her glass. He watched her lips sip the white wine.

'Interesting that we take risks to be together,' he said.

She smiled. 'But, you know, don't overthink it. Let's just enjoy these hours?'

He was on business in the city, meeting a Danish production company, but relaxing into a more clandestine purpose. In the two years since his fall on the street there'd been several incidents: one night he left the car open with the keys still in the ignition. And work was more of a challenge; only the day before, Pat had asked him how a meeting he'd left the office to go to had gone and Con just looked blankly at him. 'Oh. I completely forgot.'

Pat stared at him. 'Are you OK, boi?'

More and more he had to stop and check where he was and what he was doing. Yet his Danish dalliance continued, with meetings in different cities, using different excuses. His regular life stumbling, and his illicit life intensifying was a perilous combination. But on he went.

'Tell me about your wife,' Kirsten said, something she hadn't asked before.

It felt awkward. 'She's –'

'Have you secrets from each other?'

He thought about that question.

'You must have. I have secrets from my husband.'

'Well,' he said, 'you're *one* secret!'

'What about your wife before she met you?'

'You sound like a therapist. Ha ha!'

Amour was disrupted, but she looked at him, wanting more detail.

'Well, there are parts of her life she doesn't really talk about.'

'Interesting.'

Her furtive smile suggested the interrogation was over.

A pause, as catkins floated from above them, hitting the table with a gentle click. He wondered was he here for the adventure, or was romance's gravity trapping him on a balmy night in this fake Orient? A gentle wind blew her hair around his face as their lips touched. He drew back.

'You don't like kissing in public?' she said, feigning disappointment.

'Well,' he said, feeling her hand gently stroking his leg.

'You see, I like to get my way.' She kissed him.

'No, you don't like kissing in public,' she concluded. They laughed.

'Are you looking forward to … making love?' she asked.

'Of course.' He was trying to sound nonchalant.

Later, as Kirsten lay glowing on the bed, Con turned philosophical: 'I think one of the great things that we can do as we go through our lives … is to have close relationships with other people,' he said, trying to be profound.

'True. But tell me more,' she said.

'Well, here we are enjoying ourselves, but we know that if we told the truth at home, there'd be …' He paused suddenly.

'Go on?' she said.

Con just couldn't think of the word he was looking for. Kirsten laughed nervously.

'… turmoil … in our lives, I meant,' he said.

'So, we don't tell the truth?' she summarised, struck by the way he'd got stuck on the word. Whatever happened, it didn't stop him continuing. 'If we were both blissfully happy, we wouldn't be here, would we?'

He ventured further. 'Can you have a strings-free affair without growing an attachment to the person?'

'What do *you* think?' she asked, her breasts exposed, waiting for his mouth. 'Do you like sex with me?'

A bit of a theoretical question at a time like this, he thought.

An hour later he was alone, his lover in another bed with another person – her husband. What was *he* like, Con wondered, listening to the night sounds of a strange city; a lorry beeping as it reversed, an occasional shout, a distant train's romance. Was he in love, or had he just stepped into some fantasy land, like something from those Tivoli Gardens?

The betrayal of Fiona was troubling him, imagining her back in Cork, innocently going about her evening, looking well as she always did, maybe missing him. So why was he here? He thought of Kirsten's potency, the ecstasy of touching her, the spell her presence cast. Might she be a nightmare to live with? Yet he missed her so much now. That was it: he loved Fiona, but he *wanted* Kirsten.

Morning came, coffee wafted into the room, doors banged. He packed his things and headed to Central Station for the airport train. There was dew still on the pavements, cyclists brushed by him, the city was waking up, a Danish day getting into gear. As his train glided out of town, he nodded off. A short while later, jolted awake, he found himself in darkness, his brain labouring to catch up. Something was wrong. The train's trajectory angled steeply upwards – was it out of control? Coming out into the light, a steely-blue sea vista opened up outside the window. Still they climbed, till they were high above the Baltic Sea. A huge tanker was coming out of the mist. Confusion. Endless steel girders whizzed by. Looking up, he saw 'MALMÖ' on the LED screen over the carriage door. It was the next stop. *Sweden! Christ! The airport!*

13

Fiona woke as her train rattled and groaned approaching the platform at Heuston Station. She took the tram to Dublin city centre, then a bus north through suburbs full of memories, to her mother's house. Letting herself in, she called out from the hallway, and found her mother snoozing in an armchair in the kitchen. Jean was still living independently and loved her book club, but arthritis in her hands left the piano she loved un-played. Fiona ran her finger along a countertop and stared at the result; her mother's house pride had literally turned to dust.

A painting on the wall drew her eye, an oil on canvas, painted by Jean. It had hung there for as long as she could remember. Its view of Dublin Bay at dusk featured a larger-than-life ship; a B&I ferry to Liverpool. Jean had painted it brightly lit up, a large wash behind it suggesting determined motion. Did the vivid-looking vessel express an urge in her mother to get away, a desire that was never fulfilled?

'Oh! Darling,' her mother said, waking up. 'I nodded off there.'

'Hi, Mum!'

Her mother felt frail as they hugged but sprung as of old to put on a kettle.

'How are my adorable grandchildren?'

'Good. College seems to be going well for Ciarán. Nóra will start her nursing course in the autumn. They send their best.'

'How's Con?'

Fiona paused before she answered. 'He's away, in Copenhagen. He's fine, but do you know Mum, he's getting a bit forgetful lately.'

'Really? she said, reaching for a teapot. 'Vitamins. I bet he just needs a vitamin supplement.'

'Mum, I've a terrible feeling it might be more than that.'

Her mother seemed not to hear her. 'Let's have a nice cup of tea, Fiona?'

Fiona felt guilty for dashing away shortly afterwards, but she'd arranged to meet Deirdre. Her old friend had been through the wars, just out the other side of a broken relationship, bought a small house and wanted Fiona to see it. They'd have a girls' night out.

The house was in a little street close to the city centre. A linear park ran behind the terrace, maintained without being over-manicured, some benches that invited reflection as the city hummed in the distance. Deirdre showed her a small lake, the city reservoir from another century. Ducks squabbled on the murky brown water; a couple of drinkers, clutching their cans, argued on a bench. Their voices dropped and they nodded benignly as the two women passed.

Fiona still hadn't got the full story of Deirdre's relationship. Tonight, she was being quite tactile, touching Fiona a lot. Every time she said, 'Wait till I tell you,' she held Fiona's arm. Fiona wasn't sure how to take it; was her friend just needy?

'Is himself behaving himself, *by* himself?' Deirdre asked.

'He's away in Denmark,' Fiona replied.

'That doesn't mean he's behaving himself!'

'Who'd have him?' joked Fiona, immediately regretting the put-down.

They made their way to a traditional singing session Deirdre liked in a large Georgian house, still magnificently intact. Fiona was studying the fine flower detail of the stucco ceiling when the first singer began:

As I roved out on a bright May morning,
To view the trees and the flowers gay …

Songs of love won and lost, ballads of tyranny and treachery drew Fiona in.

'The human voice can be so intimate, can't it?' she whispered to Deirdre, struck by the way the singers' delivery brought a feeling of accord to the room.

'Yes,' Deirdre said, rubbing Fiona's arm again.

'Ok. One for the road in my place?' Deirdre suggested, when the singing concluded.

They walked up Granby Row, where elegant brick gave way to modern, nondescript architecture, then crossed Dorset

Street. They came to St Mary's Chapel of Ease, known as the Black Church. Fiona liked the lore about it. 'You will summon the devil if you run around the church anticlockwise three times at midnight. Seriously.' She told Deirdre that the poet Austin Clarke's autobiography was called *Twice Around the Black Church*. 'He was tantalising the devil with that title.'

'That's scary. It's just gone midnight,' said Deirdre, patting Fiona on the shoulder to quicken their pace.

Back in the house, she went to find some wine. Fiona followed as they talked about what her kids were up to. They were standing very close together when Deirdre handed her a glass.

'I meant to say your hair looks lovely,' she said.

Her finger touched Fiona's locks. Neither moved. Deirdre's hand was caressing more than touching.

'It's been such a nice evening,' she said.

Fiona was feeling something she wasn't sure about. Later she wondered how it happened, but their lips suddenly met.

'We're good friends, aren't we?' Deirdre said.

Fiona was about to say, 'Yes, of course,' when Deirdre's lips pressed against hers, more urgent this time. A woman desired her. How had this happened?

'Is that OK?' said Deirdre, as she took her lips away and they sat nervously with their drinks.

It was late when she turned the key in her mother's front door and crept up the stairs to her old room. It felt reassuring, safe, all ambiguity gone. Under the covers, a memory came to the rescue: she and her mother were standing looking out to sea on a lovely clear morning, islands dotted the bay in the distance. They were a couple of hundred feet up the slope of Croagh Patrick and paused to catch their breath.

Reek Sunday. Throngs of people, feet sliding on loose stones, all humanity here, some barefoot – practising a traditional route to penance. She and her mother spoke gently to each other as they climbed, exchanging a breathless word here and there. There was an unspoken solidarity in the effort it took. More than once, Fiona's hand caught her mother's as she stumbled.

'Are you all right, Mum?'

'Yes, just a little unfit.'

The last few metres of loose quartz stones were a struggle, before the cloud dissolved to reveal a bright white church at the summit, built to commemorate the place where St Patrick had fasted for forty nights.

Pilgrims buzzed around them, taking photos. Fiona remembered her mother on her knees, clutching her rosary beads and praying intensely. The summit brought a sense of being suspended between heaven and earth, of being a little closer to the former and freed from the latter (she'd read ancient holy men had this belief). She rested her elbow on her mother's shoulder, gazing at the horizon, getting perspective on the landscape, her life, the future.

'Mum. I think there's something in this …'

'Good. Wasn't it worth the effort?' her mother said, wiping her brow and gulping the water Fiona had carried to the top.

Snug under the covers now in the familiar room, but wide awake, a romantic moment early in her marriage came to mind – the time she started to write – a summer she and Con sat on a patch of pungent grass, and he'd kissed her. She could hear how the bees buzzed that day. They'd walked to a lighthouse at the southwestern end of Inis Oirr. She told him about being in the same place when she was 17. 'We were on an Irish summer course. Four of us took a walk to it, two tentative couples.'

The scene became her first creative attempt.

'We'd all read Virginia Woolf's novel, To the Lighthouse *– time passing, the complexity of being an adult, those kinds of themes.'*
'Were you in love?' he laughed.
'Something like that.'
He smiled, moved closer, and kissed her.
'Go on,' he said.
'We reached our goal, the remote white building, one of the boys thought it was a kind of milestone, so he asked the rest of us, "What do you want to do … what do you want to be?"'
The sound of a wave crashing brought her back to that teenage moment, of confidence mixed with uncertainty.
'I don't think any of us had an answer to the question.'

'Nice,' he said. 'I'm picturing you as a beautiful, inno-cent-enough 17-year-old, with adventures – good and maybe not so good – ahead of you?'

She thought for a while about the answer. 'Yes, I suppose.'

14

'Did you get the stuff?' The voice echoes around the space between a high brick wall and a moss-covered building. Con stands listening to starlings making warbles and trills on the roof. *Weren't they supposed to have inspired Mozart?*

'The stuff, Con,' says the insistent voice.

Con glances down at the bag he's carrying.

'Yeah.'

The bird chatter above them turns into a joyful song as he begins dispensing from the bag.

'Fair play to ye, boi!'

After a second night in the hostel, he'd wandered down by the river, then something drew him further east, to the old Passage West railway line, now a greenway. As he walked past Pairc Uí Chaoimh stadium, a crowd spilled out around him. 'Who were Cork playing?' he asked a man.

'Where have *you* been, boi?'

Get away from the crowd, he thought. Soon he was on a cutting, surrounded by mature trees and birdsong, before coming to an old railway platform, weeds, and moss abundant.

An old brick station building had survived the ravages of time with a trace of its former elegance intact, a forlorn reminder of its heyday. Now it was used by rough sleepers. He found an entrance and clambered in. Mattresses and sleeping bags lay scattered in the damp gloom.

A voice mumbled, 'Who's that?'

He heard an empty beer can being crushed. A haggard face stared at him before another veteran of an alternative life appeared from the shadows. They were curious about the newcomer; his speech was rambling – not that it concerned them. He didn't behave like one of the junkies with the faraway eyes they were used to. But he had cash, they discovered, and might even have a credit card. He sounded educated, a bit of a mystery, so.

Con had joined Cork's rough sleepers, a world where people come and go, on the move for different reasons. It had its own codes, which he was slowly learning. When he arrived, he asked one of the men where he was. 'For fuck's sake, you're in Cork, boi. Where'd ya tink ye were?'

Everyone laughed, except Con.

'But if you had another few bob there, I could slip around to that Spar for us?'

Con searched his pockets and found his Visa card. Security issues now eluded him. He trusted the man, Ned, who was about his age and originally from his part of the city. 'Take this and get a few things?'

An hour later, Ned was back with some bread and packs of cheese, and the card. A trust of sorts developed; now four in number, they devoured the modest food.

'You sound a bit posh for this place, Con.'

They all grinned.

Con was in a milieu he'd no experience of, apart from a few coins and a chat on the street. But the anarchy around him was compatible with where his brain, his sensibility, had ended up.

'Don't tell us you were one of those psychiatrist types?' Ned laughed.

It was time to reach for another bottle. They had alcohol – and getting hold of it – in common.

'Bring it here,' the man said, gently relieving Con of the plastic bag, the bottles rattling. Con just stood staring into the distance along the old track bed.

'Dreaming again, boi?' the man said, before turning to squeeze into the building.

A lonely feeling comes over Con now. He's thinking of the shock he got one day years before, when he lived in Dublin. His mother's voice was disjointed in panic on the phone. 'Your da … he's been taken ill.' She was swallowing a lot, a primitive whimper coming from her throat. 'I don't know what to do.'

He went pale as he looked at the receiver in disbelief. The big man had collapsed while taking his regular Sunday-morning walk. Neighbours had called the ambulance and dashed to the house. Sympathetic hands had helped, and caring eyes followed her down the road to confront the scene. The paramedics had a man on a stretcher. It was Willie, looking lifeless. They said it was his heart. Con imagined her journey, bits of Cork she knew like the back of her hand – streets, bridges, the river – flying by her, like alien places in a slow-motion blur, though the ambulance would have been speeding.

When Con reached the hospital later, his father was attached to several machines that beeped their neutral message. Doctors were doing everything they could for Willie Twomey. There were complications. With the sighs and murmurs of other peoples' crises around them, he held his mother close.

He saw Fiona alighting from the train the next day, how she lifted the gloom that followed Willie's death, he animatedly showing her the station's Victorian features, the platform for Midleton and Cobh. Driving over Christy Ring Bridge, he proclaimed: 'That's the Opera House. Dublin hasn't one, as you know.'

On the highest part of Fair Hill, he stopped the car. 'Look. I know it's not Rome, but we have our hills.' He pointed to the city in the distance, at steeples she would soon be familiar with. He looked around the modest 1950s' housing estate in which he had grown up. 'My stomping ground. We're not rich up here, but we can keep an eye on the goings on below.'

The house was full for the wake. 'This is Fiona,' he said, watching his mother's eyes settle on this woman in his life.

'I'm Máirín.'

He watched Fiona bless herself at the coffin. His mother kept gently caressing her husband's face, as if she'd a subconscious belief it could somehow bring him back to life.

At the graveside next morning, the family cast earth one by one. It smacked onto the polished wood with finality. After Con's turn, he spontaneously passed the handle to Fiona. He knew she liked ritual. He watched her work the shovel, and her piece of clay fall from the blade. They glanced at each other.

The cloudiness descends again. Where was Fiona now? He pictures a familiar road, a gate, a dark blue front door. But if he went there, he mightn't get a good reception. It was late. What would they think? Knocking on the door might wake the kids, and they'd school in the morning. He saw a woman with a scary frown. 'You were supposed to read to Ciarán tonight. He was really disappointed. Where were you?'

His brain goes blank. He shuffles around the room, perhaps once the office of a proud station master, looking for his stash of drink, bottles of Buckfast and cheap beer. The others helped themselves as he daydreamed.

'We won't let you die of thirst, boi,' a voice says.

He reaches for a bottle, screws off the cap, stares at the devout-looking monk on the label and tastes the sweetness.

15

'So, you woke up in Sweden?' the doctor said. 'What were you doing there?'

Con idly watched cars pass the surgery window. 'Eh … it was a business trip to Denmark.' He glanced at Fiona before continuing. 'Last year, strange things started happening. Things sometimes went blank, like they did that day. I ended up on that bridge to Sweden, yes. But I got the next train back to Copenhagen Airport and just made the plane.'

He laughed and started looking around him, wondering if he liked the colour of the doctor's shirt, what the paperwork on the desk was about. 'Am I losing it?' he asked.

'Let's not jump to any conclusions. How are you feeling, generally?'

'OK, but I sense slowness in the way my brain is working.'

'How would you describe it?'

'It's like a kind of … cloudiness …'

The doctor looked at them both. 'I'm going to give you a little task.'

He wrote three words on a piece of paper, asked Con to look at them, then took it back. 'When we're finished, I'm going to ask you what those three words were, is that OK?'

'That's not too hard,' Con said.

The doctor continued. 'Con, you're a healthy man, in your mid-fifties.'

Fiona mentioned pasta left cooking till it fell apart in the pot or putting the cat's bowl in the hot press.

'The cat,' Con said. He'd been worried lately about his relationship with it; he thought the tabby was staring at him with disdain, pointing at him with its black and white paws, judging him. In Con's head, a cat became a mythological creature, an ancient deity sitting aloft to deliver judgement on humankind as it erred.

'The cat can freak me out!' he said out loud.

The doctor looked him in the eye. 'What other things have you noticed about yourself lately?'

'Sometimes I go up the stairs for something and when I get there, I've forgotten what I came for.'

When it came to recalling the three words, Con hesitated. 'Window,' he said. He paused. 'Laptop!'

'And the third one?'

'I just can't remember. It slipped away somewhere,' he said, trying to make light of it.

'I think it's advisable that I refer you on,' the doctor said. Con saw Fiona's worried expression.

'OK, if you're worried about dementia, remember you're well below the age it generally gets diagnosed at.'

He told them there was a memory clinic at a city hospital. 'The team there can diagnose problems better than I can.'

It should have been reassuring but it wasn't. The doctor began preparing the referral letter. Con watched with grim thoughts, listening to the printer's neutral sound, wondering what it might be disclosing.

Walking home, he didn't want to talk. Something else was plaguing his mind – a text from Kirsten: 'How's life? You seem so far away. It would be rather nice to see you soon.'

He wanted to forget his health issues in her arms. He thought that it might be for the last time, so he needed a plan. There was the possibility of a production deal, an excuse to go to Copenhagen in a couple of weeks' time. Fiona might think it strange with a potentially serious issue hanging over him, but in the moment, he didn't care.

Tossing and turning that night, negative thoughts took over. What was happening to his memory? The pictures, the treasured songs, friendships, would all be stolen one by one, wouldn't they? To end up alone and locked in – is that what was ahead of him? How would Fiona and the kids cope?

A dream began: he could hear flight announcements, the trundle of cases and clack of heels echoing around a cavernous concourse. He stood overwhelmed, struggling to take it all in; travellers looking certain of where they were going. Kastrup Airport, Copenhagen. In a concrete railway station below the terminal building, a sleek, shiny train came to a halt with a screech. His ticket checked, the train moved through the flat suburbs, passing the skyscrapers of the extended city. After Central Station it went underground, surfacing again in the embassy belt to cruise by the beautiful houses of Hellerup and Charlottenlund.

A destination, Helsinør, appeared on a screen in the carriage. Shakespeare. That wise playwright knew humans and their dilemmas. 'To be or not to be' was only the start of it: what about the 'whips and scorns of time', the 'insolence of office'. He felt now he'd 'grunted and sweated under a weary life', as the bard said, and that 'conscience makes cowards of us all.' The words seemed to float in front of him.

The fair Ophelia! Nymph, in thy orisons
Be all my sins remember'd!

Nymph? Kirsten? He woke drenched in sweat. Then the dream resumed; he was in a hotel room, wondering why the sex wasn't proceeding smoothly; he had to think about each stage and worry that he'd manage things. It usually had its own momentum; once you were aroused, things took care of themselves. But pressure now. Kirsten wanted a satisfying orgasm and she always made sure it happened, by hook or by crook, by whatever body part worked best.

Then she appeared, looking glowing and confident at an outdoor table at an old-fashioned place he knew, Café Norden, on Østergade. He sensed her arms around him, her head on his shoulder.

'Do you know, I feel happy when I'm with you?' she said.

Then her face seemed to disappear into a crowd. He followed, bumping into people who complained in a strange-sounding language.

'You're having a nightmare, I think,' said Fiona, nudging him. 'Are you OK?'

He settled again and drifted off to sleep.

Kirsten invited herself to Ireland, in September 2017. 'I will be in London next week, so I could come to Dublin for a night, and you could meet me there?' He couldn't say no.

On the day, expectation had him strolling through the city in a good mood. Dublin looked great; the line of the quays elegant, the river calm enough to see the reflections of people crossing the Ha'penny Bridge; a busker on Merchant's Arch sounded operatic; a homeless man smiled, sage-like, as Con gave him coins; Henry Grattan looked triumphant on his plinth; weathered brick evoked Georgian elegance; the grounds of Trinity College sounded a pastoral note.

'So, this is Dublin,' she announced, alighting from a coach, and kissing him softly. 'You must give me a short tour.'

He decided the Yeats exhibition close by would be a good start. Soon they were watching the screen as famous people recited his poetry. He smiled at Kirsten as Sinéad O'Connor intoned the poet's caution for lovers:

Tread softly because you tread on my dreams.

At a pit stop in an old bar, Con waxed eloquent about the writers who drank there. He remembered one of his favourite Seán O'Casey lines as he went at his pint: 'All the world's a stage and most of us are desperately unrehearsed.'

They strolled hand in hand towards the Viking part of town. 'This is where your people settled,' he said. 'Ye came in your longboats and brought your savage ways ...'

She was ahead of him. 'You could say we have a strong seafaring legacy.'

At City Hall, he showed her the floor mosaic incorporating the city motto, *Obedientia Civium Urbis Felicitas.*

'Translate, please,' she said.

'It means ...' Con knew it well but was stuck, just staring at the words. 'You know I'm a Cork person?' he said trying to pass it off. He imagined he was back in school, and a clatter was about to come from his Latin teacher, so he'd better hurry up.

'Happy ... is ... the city ... where the citizens obey ... that's it,' he said.

'Well done.' She put her arm through his, moving closer and lowering her voice. 'But, you know, I have been getting a little ... well ... randy.'

Con didn't feel as confident at the prospect of intimacy as he used to. Yet he was willingly led to the hotel room.

'You don't seem to be your ... normal self,' Kirsten said, as she lay on the bed.

He looked at her. 'I'm having memory problems. I think there's a vitamin deficiency, or something.'

She laughed. 'So, tell me, what is my name?'

It was a relief she was making light of it.

'This part of you is working quite well, I would have thought,' she said, stroking him, already looking for more. He hesitated; her touch wasn't having the effect it always had. Was it the disease? Where were his instincts? Ecstasy was being replaced by effort.

Kirsten's phone was hopping again at breakfast; and she'd switched to business mode, frowning at the keypad. 'Problems,' she sighed, confidently tapping out a response. 'That should settle it.'

She seemed so alert and decisive at her job, he thought, envious.

'But you know ...' she said after a pause. 'I sometimes think it might be nice to disappear, to leave the world of media behind and go and make a really good wine in some sleepy village in France ...?'

'I might come too?' Con said.

The romantic thought stayed with him as they strolled to the bus stop, shared a quick kiss as the coach arrived, and he watched it disappear into the traffic.

At Heuston Station, he felt elated but a bit bereft too, missing her already. He watched the comings and goings; it wasn't Grand Central Station, but it was the busiest in Ireland, with ghosts of countless journeys, happy and sad. He climbed on board the Cork train just before it creaked and moved off. In his head he began playing out a courtroom scene. The empty seat opposite became the dock.

'Mr Twomey, could you tell the court how long your relationship with the said Kirsten Frifelt has lasted?' he heard a senior counsel boom.

Con felt like a very nervous witness. 'About two years, I think.'

'About? Surely your memory is better than that?'

'Eh … give or take a couple of months … yes.'

'Mr Twomey, we are talking about infidelity, would you not agree?' The barrister smirked.

'I suppose so.'

'Surely more than "I suppose so"?'

Moving past sidings with lonesome-looking retired rolling stock, the train whizzed through the new suburban creation, Adamstown.

'Isn't it the case that since 2015 you have deceived and lied to several parties about this relationship, principally your wife? Would you agree?'

Con hesitated and stayed silent. He looked in vain at the judge, who didn't offer any comfort.

'Mr Twomey, you must answer the counsel's question.'

Con thought about it. 'Yes, I have engaged in some deception.'

The counsel was gleeful. 'Something of an understatement I would have thought.'

Memories of last night's passion were fading. Looking out the window he saw the train had run into thick mist, fields with cattle looking ghostly. But the courtroom was vivid. The man with the posh accent and the wig continued. His witness was on the run.

'Are you in love with this woman, Mr Twomey?'

'In love? I don't know.'

Laughter broke out. Con glanced at his defence team. They looked nervy. He felt a bead of sweat roll down his forehead. What could save him from his fate? The judge summed up ponderously for the jury. The startling whoosh of a passing Dublin-bound train interrupted the proceedings.

Then he heard another voice coming from behind a trolley. 'Coffee or tea?'

'No, thank you.'

He was dozing when a cough woke him again at Mallow station; an elderly man sat down opposite him. 'A grand evening now,' the man said. As the train cleared the town, they watched the setting sun on the River Blackwater below.

'How many passengers have watched that same sun set on that river from this train?' Con wondered.

'A fair few, I'd say.'

Neither spoke for a moment, until the stranger offered, 'But it never looks the same way, always different – like the days in our lives.'

Arriving in Cork, Con felt an overwhelming feeling of exhaustion, not because of his exertions with Kirsten in

Dublin, but more because of the mental effort it was taking to be his normal self. The walk home was good; a ship's horn down river grounded him again. A saxophone shriek from a bar almost drew him in.

He opened the front door. 'Hi,' he shouted, dropping his bag.

'You're back,' Fiona called out. She asked a question that he couldn't possibly answer truthfully. 'How did you get on?'

'Good.' He was back in the courtroom again. The jury were filing in after their deliberations. The prosecution looked confident.

Fiona smiled. 'I sorted out that thing with the boiler. It was the –'

Con sighed. He looked at her features, beautiful, if ageing. *Aren't I lucky to have her?* Then Kirsten's eyes flashed in front of him – potent, alluring. How easily I could deceive, he thought. A meditation began in his head that he wasn't in control of: *is it just the sex … that won't last … was there a magic in this new woman … would I give all this up for her … maybe she'd tire of me … is sexual passion like fool's gold?*

The judge coughed and asked for the verdict. Guilty.

16

Con fixed his eyes on the sun rising inch by inch over the city. He'd wandered restlessly out to the back garden, but now he was calm. A bell rang in the distance. Even if you weren't religious, the sound was arresting, as if it was signalling something, keeping time on life, reassuring people. Dylan had a song, 'Ring Them Bells', about bells that sounded warnings, like harbingers of danger – to people, to faith, to Nature, to order.

A year and a half had passed since the first visit to the doctor. Now it was 2018. He'd been through blood tests to see if a vitamin deficiency could explain the memory loss; an MRI and then a SPECT scan – he couldn't remember the difference. There'd been an unsuccessful attempt to count backwards from one hundred in sevens, forgetting a football score from the previous day, Fiona and the doctor looking at him sombrely. He could hear the doctor's fateful words: 'Unfortunately, I am ninety per cent sure you have early-onset Alzheimer's disease.'

And then the killer line: 'The worst thing about this condition is that there is really very little we can do.'

'If it was cancer, they'd have chemo and radiation … and surgery … to try on me,' was all Con could say.

'Yes.' The doctor agreed.

Con thought of a car engine. 'Do they ever open brains up and see can they fix them?'

Now, he was worried about Nóra's reaction; she just sat in silence when they told her, tears flowing onto a textbook from her nursing course. 'Oh, Dad,' was all she could manage between sobs. He was afraid it might bring a reversal – her life was on track again after difficult years.

Ciarán, twenty-two and in his first teaching job, was analytical. 'Do you remember the afternoon we were supposed to meet in the pub before a Cork City game?'

Con vaguely recalled it.

'I rang when there was no sign of you, and you asked me … you asked me what I was doing there. You were still at home, Dad!'

Con laughed, Fiona joining in reluctantly. A doctor once told them that to get a time wrong was normal enough, to forget a whole arrangement was serious.

Con and Fiona went to tell Máirín. She was pottering around her front garden and stopped as she saw them coming up the street, calling out a welcome. 'Darlings!'

Con liked the way, at eighty-three, she still kept the house spick and span. The best cups and saucers came out. She was slowing down, a little stooped, but took pride in small rituals.

'Ma, I've got some bad news.'

'What, love?' she said, stirring the pot.

'I've been diagnosed with early-onset ... dementia.'

A cup rattled in his mother's hand. 'Oh ... love ... that's terrible.' She went to hug them both. Con watched as she and Fiona cried. It was all happening again; all the anger, sadness and bewilderment was back. Why *my* brain? How could life do this to me?

'The tea!' Máirín said, trying to be calm. As she poured, Fiona explained what they'd said at the clinic.

Máirín picked up her cup, then just stared at it before putting it down again gently to look tenderly at her only son. 'The man above works in strange ways.'

Con chose levity to drive the point home. 'You might outlive me, Mam.'

Deciding to be extra positive in the office next day, Con couldn't keep it up, and quickly turned sombre. 'I think I'll have to retire from the business.'

'You what?' Pat said, feigning surprise; he remembered only too well the woolliness, the important emails unanswered, the months of vagueness.

'Bad health news from me. It's a big problem. I've been diagnosed with Alzheimer's.'

'My God,' said Pat. 'But you're too young for *that*.'

'Early-onset, that's what I have.'

'Jesus, Con, I'm gutted.'

'That describes it. So am I.'

Con looked around the office, at photos on the wall of shoots in happier times, his arms around musicians, everybody smiling. 'I'd love to keep working, but for the sake of the business, I think I'll have to leave soon. We can work out the details later.'

'Yes, of course. How are Fiona and the kids taking it?'

Con wiped away a tear. 'They're in bits.'

'Let's have a chat over a couple of pints?' Pat had a way with him, a kindness – behind the bravado.

In the Old Reliable, where they'd shared so much craic, Con's mood was subdued. All he could do was stare at his glass. 'I still can't believe it … can't believe my bad luck. My bloody brain letting me down.'

'Maybe you'll go into remission, or something?'

'Not with this thing.'

They were the gloomiest pints they'd ever had. But Pat's TV brain was already working. The next day he had a proposal. 'I've a great idea. We should make a programme, about your experience, you know, the disease and how you're going to fight it?'

Pat didn't use the word decline, though that was what he meant.

'Make a programme out of my misery?' Con asked. He'd only seen the 'confession cam' idea used in so-called reality shows, but this was serious. Pat softened his tone. 'I know, but it's just that there's a story to be told here …?'

'Story my hole! It's all right for *you*.'

Con remembered a television programme where dementia sufferers – looking bewildered – were seated in the front row of the audience and wondered then was it exploitive. Now his own programme-maker instincts prevailed. 'How would we do it?' he said.

'You do a video diary … and later we could …'

Con knew Pat was skirting the reality, so he expressed it for him. 'You'll finish the programme when I'm gone?'

'You're going to do *what*? said Fiona that evening. 'As if we hadn't enough to deal with.'

'I felt I couldn't say no,' Con said sheepishly. 'It feels weird though.'

'I bet it does. For me, too.'

He glanced at a book she had been reading, *The Forgetting*, and felt already a goner. He opened it, flicking pages noisily, and found a section on the difference between recall and replay.

'Yes, it's interesting,' Fiona said, noticing his struggle with the text. 'Replay is what a tape recorder does; recall is a more curious skill, more sophisticated.' She took the book and read aloud, her facial expression trying to fight the gloom in the words. '"Forgetting is not a failure at all, but an active metabolic process, a flushing out of data in the pursuit of knowledge and meaning."'

'Not in this brain,' said Con, his index finger touching his skull. He could see his flippancy surprised her. 'OK. I'll make some tea so,' he said.

The next day, the idea still felt strange. Con didn't want to think where the whole thing might lead, he a living experiment, but decided to make a start. On a quiet street near his home, he took the camera out of its bag, set it on its tripod and pressed RECORD.

'I heard last night, on the BBC World Service, that in parts of Africa people with this disease are thought of as bewitched. A woman described how she travels through Nigeria trying to enlighten people, to tell them that this disease is not witchcraft.

'Then a neuroscientist said that the disease can be in your brain for fifteen to twenty years before diagnosis; abnormal proteins have been building up inside, blocking communication between neurons, that's how she explained it. And pharmaceutical companies might be bankrupt before there's a cure.

'I went for a pint and wasn't John Spillane there on a stage singing. I thought the song was about *me*!'

And your feet are drawn, down to the riverside
You sit on the stone
And you talk to the tide

Out of the blue came stuff he'd read about how tides can be capricious, malevolent, get the upper hand over human adventuring. He continued:

'I couldn't get the song out of my head the whole way home.'

Let the river go, let the river go, let the river go,
Where the river must go, let the river flow

He stopped. It felt as if a mist had descended from somewhere.

'Howya Con?' A voice called out. A neighbour looked at him curiously. 'Grand evening now?'

Con managed a mumbled greeting, before looking at the camera again.

'If I could talk to the tide, what would I say?'

17

Ned looks sceptically at Con. 'Let's go into town, lad? See can we get a few bob somewhere.'

They set off, Con with the hood of his anorak up – some instinct makes him want to be anonymous. Days have passed but he's completely lost track of time.

Ned keeps checking bins as they near the city. 'You never know what you'd find, boi.'

They're passing a jeweller's shop. Con stops to stare through the window. *I know this place.*

'What's up, boi? Do you fancy a nice watch? Ha ha.'

'Uh ... I ...'

He recalls strolling through town with his mother once, and saw the shop. 'Ma, wait a minute,' he said, disappearing through the door. He'd never bought a ring before – the choices were bewildering, but he found one he thought Fiona would like. His mother looked baffled when he emerged holding the presentation case; Con didn't discuss his love life with her. But she hoped it was for that nice girl she'd met at the wake. Fiona cried when he presented it a few days later in Rathmines, as the barmen in Slattery's congratulated them. The look in her eyes was suddenly vivid, but he could make no connection with past and present. "The perfect symbol of your endless love," the shop motto declared. Now the rows of emblems of togetherness only make him wince.

As they approach Oliver Plunkett Street, Con is reassured by a familiar sound.

'Echhh … oooo.'

A man with a bunch of *Evening Echo* newspapers under his arm calls from outside the Post Office. But the sound is like a harbinger of something, a sound from the past: maybe a foghorn through mist in Cork Harbour? A train in the distance? A sports coach calling him across a playing field in a long-for-gotten game?

Ned stands with his hand out, and his best appealing expression. 'Any chance of a few coins …?'

Con is drawn to the Liam Rúiséal bookshop's traditional front; a bottle-green weatherboard with the family name on a hand-painted sign. Something is triggered. He remembers how troublesome books had become; words seeming to move on the page, he'd be reading and forget what went before.; he couldn't separate characters in a book from real life.

The latest titles were on display; Amy Winehouse looked provocatively from the cover of one. So he started singing out loud. 'I want to keep … my dick wet …'

A man stares at him.

Con mutters. 'It's in the first verse of "Back to Black". On the recording it's hard to make out with the piano so loud.'

'Better keep it to yourself,' the man replies.

Con exits the shop and Ned grabs his arm. 'Your man over there is after giving me a tenner. He must be having a good day. I know where we'll get a few cans.'

Later, on Paul Street, Con stares at the Rory Gallagher monument, an impression of Gallagher's guitar, but distorted, looking tortured, perhaps. *Maybe it did in the end torture Rory?*

Words etched on the metal catch his eye – lyrics about the feeling of being lost and searching in the dark. Ned looks at him, starts playing air guitar – mocking him. 'Look! Wasn't this what Rory did?'

It's dusk and they're sitting with their cans near the river. Con stares at a building.

'What's up, lad?' Ned asks.

'Over there was where The Lobby Bar used to be.'

'The *what?*' Ned says, before putting the can to his lips for a good swig. 'You're a fierce man altogether for the past.'

A garda car slows down as it passes. Ned looks at Con. 'Jaysus! Maybe they're looking for *you?*'

18

July 2018. Rounding a bend, Kinsale appeared nestled in a balmy haze. Con was restless as they descended towards the town, Fiona at the wheel.

'A man could get a big thirst on him in this heat.'

'Doing your auld fella thing again?'

'But I'd love an aul pint.'

Soon the car was parked, and his pace quickened to a pub he liked. As he ordered drinks, nostalgia was triggered by the bar's music posters – Rory Gallagher in Macroom in 1977 caught his eye, bringing memories of a guitar blazing.

'I was at that one,' he told the young woman serving him. His eyes moved on, U2 jubilant in Pairc Uí Chaoimh in '87.

'That was great, too,' he said, recalling the crowd lost in the fervour that four men from Dublin created, Bono electrifying the air.

'They were at the height of their power.'

The girl continued to pour the beer without looking up, as if the swirling liquid was more interesting.

'Wow, that's a good one to have, the Rolling Stones in Cork in 1965,' he continued.

'I suppose you were at that one *too*?' she said – with a snigger.

'Am I obsessed with the past?' he asked Fiona, putting down the drinks.

'How do you mean?'

'I was just looking at posters there, reminiscing about long-ago gigs and the young one kind of slags me?' he said in a stage whisper.

'I heard her. It was a clever line. Maybe deep down you resent the suggestion you're a lot older than you think you are?'

'Maybe.'

Fiona decided to be provocative. 'Or because you still think you might have a chance with someone her age? As for your original question,' she said, taking a sip of her pint, 'remember the world moves on, and you do seem a little preoccupied with things in the past.'

'Memories come. I have no control over them. And they can bring a comforting feeling.'

The road trip was Fiona's idea, to break the gloom of the diagnosis. It would probably be the last time Con would enjoy places he liked – towns, villages, ruins, countryside. There'd be rain and sun – and recollection. She'd plotted a route, booked accommodation, got the car serviced, packed everything they'd need for the July weather. She'd a sense of optimism about the few days ahead. It might bring some of the old Con back. They'd visit places where magical days of amour, sunshine, enchantment could be summoned – she hoped.

Another part of her plan was to whisk Con's mind from the present, absorb him in the world of history and myth. The teacher had her homework done; legend and lore type books were scattered around the car so she could consult them. That afternoon she got excited rambling around the huge eighteenth-century Charles Fort, outside the town. 'Have you heard about the tragic bride of Charles Fort, the White Lady as she was called?' she asked.

'Why was she tragic?'

'It was a case of mistaken identity, and brutal military code. She's supposed to haunt this place in her white dress.'

She decided to cut a long story short. 'Her father, a senior officer at the fort, shot the soldier she was due to marry, after finding him asleep on his watch. He didn't realise in the darkness it was his son-in-law to be. But death was the penalty.'

They looked out on the mass of stone. Crows perched harmlessly on the stoutly built battlements.

'It gets more tragic.'

'What happened?'

'The father killed himself. Then she, in grief, threw herself off one of those ramparts.'

'So, it was love that drove her to that.' Con said.

Later, they stood admiring the view of the harbour from their room. He thought of seafaring adventure, salty air on the nose, watching a yacht leaving the inner harbour, carving a wake in the still water. Where was it heading? He watched it till it melted into the evening; a harbour can make you dream.

Fiona propped herself on the bed, comfortable with her book, an engrossed expression on her face. It was *The Bell Jar* by Sylvia Plath.

'Remind me what the bell jar means?' he asked.

'It's like the bell jar in chemistry class in school. Remember? It sucks air out to create a vacuum.'

'So, what's the ... significance?' He had to find the word.

'Well, the jar is sucking the air, the reason to go on, from the heroine's life.'

He was looking out the window again, watching the light disappear from the harbour, being sucked away by the night. Subdued, he quietly joined Fiona in bed. The amorous mood they'd felt on the walk home was gone. He was asleep shortly afterwards.

Wide awake now, inspired by memory, Fiona took out her notebook. The pen scraped vigorously on the paper.

You expected music to burst from the potent-looking timber buildings; yet a hint of menace came from an unseen world of poverty close by; unkept streets, curious looks from wizened men, coffee you could chew on; clapboard shacks, oceans of crops, still air, frogs hopping, moans and hollers imagined. Good memories of a place. But uneasy ones; a romance that went west, and the consequence of it that would remain my secret.

She put down the pen. Could she tell Con about all that pain *now*? Maybe she had to?

The road next morning took them into a lush valley, to a magical lakeshore. Gougane Barra. The sound of the car doors closing echoed in the air. Water lapped, craggy rocks and pine trees rose above them as they set off walking.

Con pointed out the tranquil-looking small island. 'St Finbarr built his first church, in the ... eighth century, would it have been?'

'I think the sixth century.'

She knew the saint's history. 'The monks knew how to pick their spot. Location, location. It mattered for devotion too.'

'What is it about ancient Christianity you like so much?' he asked.

'It's the physical evidence of belief, and its endurance,' Fiona said, her eyes twinkling. A cascading stream in the distance made her think of a verse from her schooldays.

In deep-valley'd Desmond, a thousand wild fountains,
Come down to that lake from their homes in the mountains.

Sitting down to lunch in Cronin's café, they ordered vegetable soup. Everything was fine till Con fell silent and seemed confused by the food in front of him, brown bread, butter, and a bowl of broth. He put the piece of wrapped butter into the soup, realised his mistake and tried to retrieve it.

Fiona pretended not to notice.

Driving back towards the main road, she kept slowing down and looking around her.

'Mind the road, Missus!'

She told him she was looking for a ruin: the house where *The Tailor and Ansty*, a banned book in the 1940s, was set.

'Do you remember the Tailor's motto?' she asked, noisily finding a higher gear and abandoning the search. '"Take the world fine and aisy and the world will take you fine and aisy." Good advice, isn't it?'

Con was silent again.

In Kenmare, they found the well-cared-for period house Fiona had booked, so somewhere to have a couple of drinks was next.

'I'm not interested in a place that has a sign saying, "*ceól agus craic*". I want a *real* pub', said Con, cranky as he vetted exteriors. Soon, he sat contented with a pint in a convivial pub, as a group of musicians played. Somebody sang 'The Banks of Sullane,' a Munster song he liked. An American tried 'Ride On'. The musicians launched into a set of reels just as he finished, in case he'd sing another.

It was midnight when they strolled back to the guest house.

'I'd love to do a music pilgrimage to the southern states of America,' Con announced.

'Where did that notion come from?' she was a little freaked. This was far from her favourite subject.

'You never told me much about your time there?'

The question felt like a prod to Fiona. He continued. 'I'm hearing slide guitars in my head and Black men with gravelly voices.'

On the spur of the moment, to humour him, she decided to offer some amiable recollections of that summer of 1984.

'There was a place in Clarksdale you'd love.'

'Give me pictures,' he said.

Rising to the challenge, she continued. 'I can still hear the sound of the railroad bells, and see lights flashing, real Americana.' She was warming to her subject. 'I remember standing at a level crossing in a dodgy, beat-up part of town. A hooter sounded; an engine roared.'

'That's good. Go on.'

'The hooter sounded like someone playing a giant harmonica – badly. Then came the longest train you'll ever see. It groaned and rattled, with every tone that could be got from steel meeting steel. It took at least five minutes for the wagons to pass.'

'The railroad is the sound of America to me. I can hear it now. Go on.'

'The train disappeared into the distance and the evening silence returned. We carried on down Sunflower Avenue, looking for a place we were told about on the corner with Martin Luther King Drive, a juke joint called Red's.'

'There must have been noises?'

'A dog barked in the distance; a bullfrog croaked some-where in the tufts of grass between the rails.'

'That's what I wanted to hear,' he said, his eyes closed in a trance.

'On we went. James, the fella I was with, kept saying it had to be a proper juke joint, the real thing. We did a lot of walking. We'd been to the Robert Johnson Crossroads earlier that day. The scene we looked for seemed hard to find, even in a place like Clarksdale, with all its history.'

They came to a small, early-twentieth-century brick building. Inside, it was well-worn, dark and not very clean, cluttered with old refrigerators, propane tanks and bits of wrecked furniture, but atmospheric.

'I remember the man behind the bar, just saying "white folk". It was "Red" himself – his way of greeting. "We'll have two beers," James said, trying to be confident. The bottles were opened and smacked down on the bar. We asked if there was music later. "Not till dark," we were told. A tall Black man with white shirt and flamboyant tie took to the stage a couple of hours later and plugged in his guitar. "Hello, y'all," he said, as his fingers danced along the frets, checking his sound.'

'Electric Blues ... great!' Con interjected.

'An elderly man leaned over to tell us it was Big Jack Johnson. "He's a regular here. They call him 'oil man' because he drives a goddamn big tanker," he added with a smoker's wheeze.'

Con asked her if she could remember any of the numbers.

'There was one was called "I'm Your Oilman".'

'How did it go?'

'About being an oilman and wanting to come on your mountain … that kind of thing – primeval imagery,' she laughed. 'Let me change your oil … or words to that effect.'

'Sounds good,' Con said. 'But you still never told me where that lad James got to?' 'No idea,' she deflected, secretly relieved she'd avoided telling him about the Mississippi experience that she *really* remembered – the awkward conversations, the uncomfortable meals shared, the unpredictability of James beside her in bed, the strange sounds in the dead of night. No, sex that time wasn't funny.

19

There was no escaping the rain; it blocked light like a veil, blew through the town in sheets, overloading drains, cold and unrelenting, making everyone cross in its wake. It felt as if all of Kerry was saturated, never to be dry again.

'It was grand up till this morning,' the guest house owner repeated, as if she felt obliged to save Kerry tourism all by herself.

Something else had Con in bad form: he'd noticed a book Fiona brought, with a scary cover, a graphic of a tree in the shape of a human head. Part of the tree was denuded, leaves floating away, a section of the branches ominously bare. She was in the shower when he opened it on the Preface, and a grim passage: "I remember watching the brilliant light that echoed from my grandfather's soul dissipate into absolute and irrevocable darkness."

He skipped on a few paragraphs. It didn't get any better – he scanned phrases like 'failed clinical trials' and 'reduced cognitive performance'.

'You brought some light reading?' he said when she came back into the room.

His look made her change the subject. 'Listen to that rain!'

Fiona could barely see the road as she drove out of the town. Signposts offered options of places that were already drowned in rain or mist. To a soundtrack of tyre meeting water, they headed out on the famous road loop, the Ring of Kerry.

'Isn't it only a little drop of rain,' Con mocked. 'They have to play it down around here. It's just a once-off, really – the sun will be out any minute.'

In Waterville, Charlie Chaplin's statue glistened in the wet. They strolled down the modest seafront the retired film star would have walked during his many holidays in the village.

'Did he hold his wife's hand? Did he make funny faces or shout at the kids?' Con wondered.

Walking towards a spot on the beach lit by a shaft of sunlight, he stopped to watch a man and two children pulling a small boat towards the sea. Their progress fixated him, their optimism that the rain was gone. The kids shrieked, the man snapped orders, their dog made a fruitless dash after a seagull. Time passed. Someone called his name. Fiona was running towards him, blowing out a series of small breaths. 'Why did you disappear on me like that?'

He didn't respond. Flashes from holiday scenes long ago were congested in his head, tormenting him. She gently took his hand.

The day had turned idyllic as Fiona read the plaque at The Tetrapod Trackway on Valentia Island. 'Fossilised footprints from 385 million years ago; a primitive amphibian-like creature left its footprints on a piece of mud. They became fossilised, a process that took thousands and thousands of years.'

Con had to think. 'I see a creature wailing, with leathery scales oozing liquid, leaving its mark for tourists of the future.'

'That's it,' she said, linking his arm. 'What mark will *we* leave, do you think?'

He looked at her wanting to respond, but nothing would come.

Con took in the Killarney hotel room's elegant furniture, antique bed, crisp linen. 'Creature comforts – at last,' he purred.

But he was restless and decided to set off exploring. Fiona said she'd take a bath.

'I'll follow you later,' she said. 'Take your camera?'

He was drawn to the red brick station building, the robust cast-iron roof and timber canopy marks of the golden railway era. He found a seat and extracted the camera from the bag, looked sceptically at it, and pressed RECORD.

'It's a few days into our holiday. I'm feeling OK, mostly. Fiona is taking care of me, of course. We're having some nice times together. But I hesitate in the middle of a conversation, looking for a word ...'

He paused, looked around him and gazed at the tracks stretching into the distance.

'I keep thinking I can hear the rails in all those train songs …'

Staring at a poster, 'Rediscover Ireland – by Train,' he was back on holiday long ago. His father and mother brought him camping to Killarney when he was seven. They came by train. He was still lost, remembering, as Fiona appeared at his side.

'What are you thinking?'

'My poor mother, how she struggled with us in primitive conditions. We were in an old tent, which was fine till the rain came. We were soaked but we managed. It was happy, we laughed, so why do I just remember the rain?'

'Is it a nice memory, though?'

'Yes, except I can hear the rain on the canvas, see it seeping under the wall of the tent. I think of my father carting the rolled-up tent, moist and smelly, to the platform. We waited for the train to take us to Mallow and then home. Dampness and happiness are my memories of that holiday.'

'How was your dad then?'

'My mother and father seemed happy. I think it was when he'd kicked the drink.'

'That's nice.'

Con kept staring at the people at the next table when they sat down to dinner.

'What's wrong?' Fiona asked.

'Why can't people learn to use a knife and fork properly?'

'Yes, but why let it bother you?'

He raised his voice. 'I-must-not-hold-my-knife-like-a-pencil – do you remember that? Simple rule. We were always taught it. And we weren't posh, as you know.'

The man was scooping food onto the front of the fork with his knife.

'Feck that!' said Con. 'It's a restaurant, not a building site!'

A waitress arriving with a bottle of wine distracted him.

'How are you feeling these last few days?' Fiona said as she watched the drink settle in her glass.

'Sometimes I feel great. I even think about making a full recovery. Then the cloudy feeling comes back, and I have to think for a second where I am.'

'Do you know, despite what I was saying to you, I'd be lost without you,' she said.

A tear came. 'That's so sweet of you.'

Was this her moment? It might well be their last weeks with Con in any kind of equilibrium. The subject had already been broached the night before. Something told her this was the time.

'Con, do you remember we were talking about America last night and you were asking about James?'

'Yes.'

'Well, it was … an unhappy time in my life, really. That's why … I haven't talked about it. What happened then I've just kept to myself. I know that seems strange, given how long we've known each other, that I've kept a secret from you for so long.' She smiled tenderly, but his face was deadpan.

'Secret? Go on,' he said.

She was nervous now. 'James and I began to quarrel a lot that summer.'

'And?' Con sounded irritated.

She wondered how she'd go on. 'He had … he had a violent streak …'

'Drink?' Con asked, frowning.

'It was to do with …' Her voice lowered. '… sex.'

The look on Con's face made her wonder if she had done the right thing.

He put his glass down hard. But it was the way he raised his voice that most startled her. 'I don't like the sound of this. *Then* what happened?'

'Things got worse, then we went our separate ways. It was a very unhappy time.' She reached for his hand. 'I just wanted to tell you …there's more …'

'I think I've heard enough.'

A voice relieved the tension. 'Can I get you anything else?'

Con fidgeted with his napkin, looked away from Fiona, throwing a scowl across the room. 'You could ask that fella to put away his shovel?'

'Con!' Fiona said.

His static look returned, as if animation was being held up by something. All she could see now was vulnerability, a creased face, sadness in his eyes, fidgety hands, the confidence that she always loved drained from him.

'Let's go up to that nice old pub around the corner and get you another pint before bedtime?' she said.

How patronising it sounded, she thought afterwards, watching Con's first sip. There was no look of expectation as his lips closed in on the drink; he seemed indifferent. What had she started? Had she picked the right moment – was there any right moment?

Calm had returned as they lay in bed.

'What are you reading?' he asked.

'More *light* reading, I'm afraid.'

'Read a bit, so.'

'OK,' she said, flicking pages. 'It says here, "As gravity holds matter from flying off into space, so memory gives stability to knowledge …" It's from Ralph Waldo Emerson.'

She assumed he took the quote to be a reference to their earlier discussion when he let out a sigh. 'A little knowledge can be a dangerous thing,' he murmured, putting an arm round her.

20

Fiona slipped out of bed in the half light, floorboards creaking as she tiptoed from the room. A cough came faintly through a wall, a door banged somewhere. She was making her way out to walk the town, alone with her thoughts and the stillness.

Two crows squabbled on The Square. Without traffic and people, it could have been Listowel in another era. She thought of the town's ghosts, its dead writers. She came to the statue of John B. Keane, arm outstretched, in full flow as if sharing some anecdote or wisdom. Starlings flew around him, as if in homage. The characters that inspired him came from the shops, pubs, streets, and farms outside the town.

The sad, the eccentric, the joyous minds of his characters always impressed her: the troubled father in *The Year of the Hiker* was one. A man returns to his family after abandoning them for twenty years. Keane keeps the audience guessing as to why – was it the man's mental state? Then comes the revelation – a secret Keane keeps artfully for dramatic effect. So, would she try again to make *her* revelation?

As they drove north, Con sang odd lines from songs. One struck Fiona. 'That's Joni Mitchell, "Refuge of the Roads," isn't it?'

'Yes. She leaves the fella and takes to the road – to escape.'

'Maybe a more romantic road than this one?' she chipped in.

'All roads have their stories, even this one.' Con said, staring absently ahead.

'She wrote so well about restlessness, breaking free, open spaces, desert, and skies … the romance of the road?'

He wasn't really following her now.

She could hear another Mitchell song, about love, winning and losing it, finding paradise, or coming to harm, metaphors about aviation, skies, falling, crashing, false alarms – in love and elsewhere. She knew all about that.

Glancing at Con, a warm feeling came – what was it about him she loved? Just *him*, really – his nature, the years of contentment, the bond, or was it the mystery of attraction, a biological thing …? How would their love endure through his illness?

The car started to drift over the white line.

'Watch out!' Con shouted, as a long horn blare came from another car.

She took a deep breath. 'Sorry.'

After crossing the Shannon by ferry, they passed through towns and villages set among rolling hills: Kilrush, Cooraclare,

Quilty, Miltown Malbay, Lahinch, Liscannor. The bustle of summer played out; bed-and-breakfast signs, menus on boards, ice-creams, with or without a Flake, buckets, spades, children on holidays, towels on a beach and waves crashing – motifs of an Irish summer holiday.

'You came here a lot making programmes, didn't you?' Fiona said.

Con was silent, as if listening to the engine's tones. 'Do you see the sun?' he said suddenly, staring at the sky.

'What about it?'

'It's getting ready to slide down over the Atlantic.'

Banal but sweet, she thought, the man she loved struggling bravely against a disease.

Climbing towards the Cliffs of Moher, she remembered Saint Brigid's Well and pulled in at the place of pilgrimage, where a plaster image of the saint kept vigil.

'I won't be a minute,' she said, pulling the handbrake. She slipped inside the narrow, cave-like grotto, where rosary beads, Mass cards and messages pleaded for intercession from the saint. Faded pictures of deceased loved ones all around her were reassuring evidence of old belief, before her own prayer, for Con's recovery.

At the cliffs, she watched birds glide elegantly on the air currents, so at ease where humans couldn't go. They walked south, to where the flagstone barriers ended. Waves broke far below, the distance delaying the sound of each breaker. But Con was straying too close to the edge.

'Con, *stop!*' She lunged to grab his hand. He grinned at her as she pressed her free palm to her heart, aware she'd panicked.

'Do you remember Dusty Springfield?' she asked, trying to hide her alarm. 'She requested half her ashes be scattered here,' she said, imagining the great voice soaring – like the seabirds now.

'I'll Close My Eyes and Count to Ten. Isn't that the one?' he said, before starting to sing jumbled lines about pounding-in-the-heart.

'Stop, you're annoying me,' she said.

They went back to the car and drove on in silence.

At Doolin, she changed into her swimsuit and ran to the sea, hitting the cold foam and plunging in. Con walked to the edge and watched her. When she left the water and came up the sand, he took in her shape, a little heavier now than when they first met, but still very attractive. A strong urge to kiss her came. Observing her attempt at modesty, struggling to get out of wet togs and back into clothes while wrestling with a towel, he began fantasising about a young Fiona. It's the context – open air, the beach; it makes people skittish, he thought. Maybe the feelings were something more problematic, he wasn't sure.

Soon they were checking in to the old-world Falls Hotel in Ennistymon, the avenue lined with magnificent trees. A plaque in the lobby and photos recorded it as once the family home of Dylan Thomas's wife, Caitlín McNamara. She'd worked in the bar while her father converted the house to a hotel.

Fiona knew some of the story. 'What an amazing couple: alcoholism, infidelity and God knows what else. Always broke, his poetry took him away on tours to America, he drank stupidly, had affairs, while she was stuck at home with three kids, but they were still in love when he died. Epic!'

'Let's go up the town for a pint?' Con suggested, as if he hadn't heard her.

Crows flew noisily from the huge sequoia trees on the avenue as they strolled towards the main street.

'What is it about crows, like they're an omen of something?' said Fiona.

'Of what?'

'How would I know,' she laughed. 'It just sounds good. Could be a poem from somewhere, Dylan Thomas, even?'

He stopped to listen to the birds.

'What's the collective noun for crows, teacher?'

'A murder.' She grabbed his hand to hurry him along.

'It's so quiet I can hear the Guinness pouring into the glass,' Con said when they got to the pub.

He was in good form. Was it her chance? Then Con began studying the posters lining the walls, for a folk festival from nearly forty years before, now part of local legend.

'I was there in 1983,' said Con. 'Van and Rory headlining – and the Hell's Angels running amok.'

'And worse,' said the man.

'Yes. I remember; eight young fellas were drowned,' Con said.

'Awful. Just going for a swim. That was the end of it,' the man said stoically.

They sipped their drinks. In a corner a woman started playing a concertina, notes swirling around the bar like glitter.

Fiona touched Con's arm. 'Do you remember what I was telling you the other night about James, and that time?'

He looked at her puzzled.

'The conversation we started, at dinner?'

The music was preoccupying him. 'What conversation?'

'I was telling you …'

'Isn't that music *so* sweet?' he said. 'She's making the notes *float*.'

The other matter was superseded. Fiona nudged Con's arm. 'Like grace notes – from Heaven?' she said.

Later in the room, she found it hard to wind down. She felt amorous too.

'This afternoon … when I was swimming … you were –'

'Yes.'

'Well …' She put her hand gently on his leg.

Con's head was on the pillow, his eyes closing. Years ago, at moments like this, passion could flare, tenderness and the erotic meeting. Where had it gone? She went to brush her teeth, turning the bathroom light on. The face looking back from the mirror took her a little by surprise. The light flattered her, she thought, turning to scrutinise her profile. Yes, eyes were her best feature. Her chin didn't stick out too much and her skin was doing a good impersonation of a forty-something-year-old. *I'm not unattractive.*

She switched off the mirror light, but more reflection came. Was it a good idea to bring up events in America over thirty years ago? She was only 21 then; James cut a dash; she was in love. His assurance and confidence seduced her – as did blues music's artifice. Thinking of the dark side of that time brought a shiver. *Can't we be so easily led?* She remembered one of the bad nights; without warning he just pushed her onto the bed, a scowl on his face. He tugged at her clothes. 'James, what's wrong?' she said in vain, as his hand creeped. She could still feel the mustiness in that room, his grabbing hands.

The window was open to the balmy air. Looking out to the dark grounds, she thought of the murder of crows – all asleep in the trees now. Thomas's poem, 'Do Not Go Gentle into that Good Night' came to her, the poet's rage about light disappearing.

Climbing into bed, she saw Con's phone light up. *Who'd be texting him this time of night?*

21

Kirsten Frifelt watched another sunset over Copenhagen's western suburbs, accompanied by a familiar, restful sound, the rumbling of an S-train a couple of streets away. In a park across the street, the sun's last rays illuminated life scenes: children and dogs acting up and being corrected; one couple on a bench arguing, another kissing; a worker slowly pushing a barrow.

She'd lived in this third-floor apartment in Frederiksberg since she'd married fifteen years before, meticulous about the upkeep of the five rooms in the stylish, well-maintained building. Paintings by her husband hung on the wall; one was a scene imagined in the Christiania hippy commune begun in the 1970s, in the old military area on the other side of town. Figures with long hair stood around smoking, but there was something darker about the picture, the suggestion that maybe peace and love was not nirvana. On another wall, a surreal take of the city's famous Round Tower on Købmagergade; fairy-tale figures flew around its wall as if in homage to the seventeenth-century building.

Her years here had been mostly happy; she and her husband, Erik, were comfortably off, both had fulfilling careers. The effort Kirsten put into the smooth running of the household didn't stop her recalling the secret, more adventurous side of her life, wondering why she hadn't heard from her Irish lover in a while. She relished their meetings, one not far from where she stood now. It was risky – but she had confidence in the anonymity of Copenhagen's size.

Her view of the relationship was practical; it wouldn't get out of hand; she could manage her emotions – like one of her productions – coolly and calmly. Con was a good diversion from the routine of work and home. They liked each other's company – no harm in that? She wasn't going to leave her family for a long-distance relationship.

It was a thing about tall men, they were potent when it came to sex, she believed, and Con was skilful; if all else failed, his lips could deliver. She often wondered if hers was a recreational attitude to sex, something to turn on or off as she pleased, like music, perhaps. But men could do it, so why not her?

The last time they'd met she'd noticed changes; he could take unusual turns in a conversation; there was unpredicta-bility in intimacy, too. Perhaps it made him more alluring? She'd decided to message him, with a furtive suggestion.

The setting sun was slowly reducing people in the park to silhouettes, as if their animation was being drained.

'A glass of wine?' a voice said. It was Erik, who appeared from the room he used for writing. He stood beside her now.

'Must be interesting?' he said, noticing her far-away look.

She gave him the wide-eyed look and a grin he liked; it usually meant she'd sorted it out, whatever it was. He seemed in a good mood – that often came when he'd a productive day writing.

Soon, the cork popped on a bottle of Sancerre, and he was pouring gently. Kirsten thought he'd become a little obsessive, swirling and sniffing, commenting each time he took a sip.

'I get grapefruit strongly in this one,' he said.

'Yes, but whatever, it has a Friday feeling,' she said.

She looked at him. His dress sense was both annoying and endearing, a scruffy look, the expression of an artistic foible, she accepted. His trousers were far too big and trailed on the floor, his shirt hanging loose. Bohemian, even for Copenhagen.

Looking down to the street she saw Anders, their son, dismounting his bike. He waved up looking carefree. A few minutes later, the apartment door opened.

'Hi!' he said, then he'd disappeared into another room. Loud sounds from a keyboard followed.

'He's a dreamer, that boy,' Kirsten said.

'He takes after me, I suppose,' Erik said. 'Isn't he playing with his band this weekend?'

'I think so. How was your day?' she asked.

'Good. I think I've sorted out the motivation for the dark turn my central character takes.'

'Oh. Interesting.'

'It's connected to his wife's infidelity,' he said.

The music stopped. Anders put his head around the door and saw the glasses of wine. 'Can I have some?'

'I'll get you a glass,' Erik said padding back to the kitchen.

As he picked up the chilled bottle, Kirsten's phone twitched on the table where she'd left it, beside her laptop. Words about the rocky landscape of the west of Ireland, packaged and encoded so the cell network could understand them, acknowledged, and relayed over hundreds of kilometres, were now vibrating on the wood. Erik picked up the phone and handed it to Kirsten when he returned to the living room. She looked at it, wondering if he'd noticed the words in English on the screen.

22

On the Long Walk in Galway, Fiona stood observing the tide. 'Amazing, isn't it? Millions of cubic metres of water, moving silently round the earth, on a twice-daily schedule, six hours one way, six hours the other,' she said, turning to Con.

'You know I love tides,' he said.

They gazed across the stillness to The Claddagh.

'Do you remember reading *Rain on the Wind*?' she asked, eyes fixed on the distance.

'Remind me?'

'It's a story of love and nature. The fishermen struggle against the weather, the sea, and poverty. The central character, Mico, has a prominent birth mark – like a cross he must bear.'

'You like crosses,' he smiled. And what happens?'

'He tries to find love. But it gets complicated. And the elements, the things that can't be controlled, always threaten.'

Two swans went by, contented-looking veterans of the water's movements.

'We better go,' she said.

It was the middle of their road trip, and they'd arranged to meet Deirdre, in Tigh Neachtain, one of Galway's lived-in pubs. Since their night out in Dublin, there'd only had sporadic contact, and though she looked forward to seeing her friend, she was nervous too.

'What's Deirdre been at?' Con asked.

'She's teaching in a school here and living with her new partner, Pauline.'

In the pub, Fiona was admiring sorcerous-looking figures on an old Arts Festival poster when someone called her name. She turned around and Deirdre hugged her, a long embrace. She wondered if Con had noticed.

'This is Pauline,' Deirdre said. 'Pauline, an old friend of mine, Fiona, and her husband, Con.'

Fiona sensed Pauline scanning her as if she might be a threat.

'Good to meet you at last,' Fiona said, giving both the obligatory kiss on the cheek.

Con just said hello, always cooler with women he didn't find attractive – a macho trait. Fiona wondered if he'd notice any awkwardness between her and Deirdre and just wanted the gathering to be convivial. Con got the ball rolling. 'Same again?' he said, looking at Deirdre and Pauline's near-empty glasses. 'Con Twomey won't let anyone go thirsty.'

'It's really good to see you,' Deirdre said, rubbing Fiona's arm. 'How's the holiday going?' She looked round to make sure Con wasn't nearby. 'How's he doing?'

'Fine, mostly,' Fiona confided, out of Pauline's earshot. 'A bit unpredictable, sometimes you get the old Con and sometimes the changed Con, but the trip is doing us good, we're enjoying it and I don't want to think too far ahead. So, how have you both been?' she said, glancing at Pauline.

'We're exhausted, from the campaign,' Deirdre said.

The referendum to repeal the Constitutional amendment preventing abortion legislation had been passed by a substantial majority of Irish citizens at the end of May. Activism was part of the relationship, Fiona guessed.

'Defeat for the Church,' said Pauline triumphantly, assuming any friend of Deirdre's would automatically concur with her.

Fiona rose to the challenge. 'Lots of practising Catholics voted yes, remember? Otherwise, it wouldn't have passed.'

There was tension in the air. Fortunately, Con came back with the first two pints. 'Did I hear the word "referendum" just now?' he said jovially, as he put down the drinks and went back to get the other two. 'Can we agree that it should never have been in the Constitution in the first place?' he added, in a moment of lucidity as he set the remaining drinks on the table.

'I voted to allow the introduction of abortion. I thought it was the right thing to do – for the country,' Fiona said.

'It was a great victory. We've been enslaved too long,' said Pauline.

Fiona looked at Con and rolled her eyes. Fortunately, a man with a guitar started playing near them, his PA turned up to get attention. When he got stuck into his version of 'Galway Girl' conviviality was restored and more pints were had.

Fiona was exercised on their way back to the guest house. 'That righteousness really gets to me,' she said.

The river was angry now as it tumbled into the harbour at low tide. A nice distraction. Fiona stopped to read the poem by Moya Cannon set in stone on the bridge. 'It's subtle, contemplative, not like all that doctrinaire guff we heard from Pauline tonight.'

She read aloud in the dim light, lines about five swans making their way across the bay, carrying the world's beauty on their strong white backs.

'You didn't take to Pauline?' said Con.

'Bit of an ideologue, I thought.'

Fiona was struck more by the way Con mostly stayed out of the discussion. He used to enjoy giving his opinion, hopping balls. But not anymore. It was as if he hadn't followed the thread of the chat. Will a tipping point come in his condition, and how will we know? She fretted. He was her soulmate, she felt tenderness towards him, making her put her arm around him protectively now. She didn't want him to sense her anxiety.

The following morning, there was no hanging around drinking more coffee at breakfast. Fiona wanted to visit the cathedral before they left, to see the Stations of the Cross again.

First, they rang home to check on the kids. Ciarán answered. 'Hi, Ma. How are things going?'

'We're having a great time. Is everything OK? How's Nóra?'

'Fine.'

'Any post?'

'A couple of official-looking ones, bills I think, and there's a wrecked envelope that's been re-addressed a couple of times. Looks like it's been around the world.'

'I'll see it when we're back.' Her stomach heaved. It might be the letter she thought might arrive *someday*.

She was pleased to reach the rarefied sanctuary with its beautiful Connemara marble floor. They stopped at the Second Station, Christ Carrying the Cross, carved, like the others, out of Portland Stone by the artist, Gabriel Hayes, in eighteen years of work.

'The stations are a reminder of the final days of Jesus's life, when he had to contend with injustice, hatred and betrayal. That's why the Stations are so important,' Fiona said, in a whispered fervour.

She looked intensely at the depiction of Jesus. 'You see, we all have crosses to bear in our lives.'

When Con wandered into a side chapel, Fiona went to light a candle – her private moment. Watching the gentle flame melt the wax, she thought about what that letter might contain.

The days in Galway and Mayo seemed to blend and soon they were heading south towards home. Con became odder; at Clonmacnoise, he stared for ages at a pilgrim sculpture at the visitor centre, apparently intrigued by the figure's hand covering its face.

'You see, no eyes,' he said. 'So, faith can be blind, Fiona?'

After making her own short pilgrimage among the monastic ruins, she found Con sitting on the grass beyond the main site, staring towards the Shannon. Sun shone on the water, the river almost lake-like at this part of its course. She watched for a while, then looked at him. What was going on in that head?

'I'm watching the river flow,' he said. 'Like Bob Dylan did.'

She laughed. 'It doesn't do much flowing around here.'

'It flowed for me just now.'

The last stop on their road trip was a walk on the largest remaining raised bog in Ireland, near Clara, Co Offaly. Timber planks on the wooden walkway moved underfoot. There was silence, except for birdsong – wildlife came into its own in this special place. It was better than a retreat. Fiona heard a curlew, recognising its distinct call from her childhood. The beautiful notes of a lark stirred Con, out here on the bog, with nothing for miles, the absence of people, he couldn't believe how pure it sounded.

'Bogs are great preservers of things, like bodies from ancient times, buried books, trees, treasure troves,' Fiona said.

Con, without warning, suddenly took his foot from the walkway and stuck it into the peaty water below, a squelching sound amplified by the stillness of the place.

He retrieved the wet limb and stared at it. 'Do you remember what Seamus Heaney asked? How could a preserved body be referred to merely as a corpse?' He started to recall phrases – the poet's marvel at the vitality of the preserved figure, in turf for millennia.

Fiona knew the poem, 'The Grauballe Man'. 'How do you remember those lines?' she asked him.

'I don't know. My memory is playing all kinds of tricks on me.'

'What about your video diary thing – since you're in full flow?' she laughed. She wondered what he'd come out with, given the way his memory was behaving; lines of poetry flowing and yet he can't follow a conversation. She loved him, but was this the future?

He scowled. 'Ah … I'll leave it.'

The M8 cut through the Golden Vale, and soon they were descending into the Jack Lynch Tunnel and Cork city at rush hour. Exiting the South Ring, they could see St Finbarr's Hospital, the buildings an uncomfortable reminder of another reality.

Ciarán and Nóra had dinner ready, a chickpea curry, with red cabbage sautéed in mustard seeds and turmeric, and basmati rice. Máirín had come to join them.

'Well done. Getting rice right can be tricky,' Fiona said.

'Do ye like me cooking, Dad?' Nóra teased, looking for praise.

He had to think about the question. 'It was … terrific!'

'Thanks, Dad,' though she wasn't sure if he remembered what he'd eaten.

They began recalling holidays. 'Remember the caravan park in Glenbeigh when it rained the whole week?' Nóra said. 'I thought I'd go mad.'

'It didn't rain the whole week,' Ciarán countered. (He'd fallen in love among the anchored mobile homes, remembered walking hand in hand with someone on a long, golden beach in his memory, only a gentle, salty breeze to get in the way).

'Ciarán, do you remember the day Sheppy – the poor dog was losing it then – decided to just swim straight out from Inchydoney Beach?' Nóra asked. 'And Dad, you just jumped in and swam after her, and we watched you came out of the waves with her – a hero,' she added.

Con looked puzzled.

Máirín stood up. 'It's way past bedtime for me.'

Fiona walked with her to the bus stop, knowing she'd want an update on Con's condition.

'God love him, Fiona,' she said, as they crossed the street. 'How was he on the holiday?'

'Up and down, really.'

Fiona was thinking of all the incidents but kept it to generalisations. 'He's becoming more unpredictable.'

Máirín clutched her handbag tightly before her next question: 'He hasn't been violent though, has he? That can happen.'

'No, thank God.'

'I never told you about the time his father was drinking?'

A bus approached so Fiona put her hand out, reluctantly, given the turn in the conversation.

'We'll talk about it again,' said Máirín as she boarded slowly.

Fiona watched her find a seat before the bus moved off with a roar. She stood thinking of Máirín's independence, admiring her her mental ability at such an advanced age. It's interesting the way memories survive and surface unexpectedly like that, Fiona thought.

Back at the house, Nóra handed her a bunch of envelopes. 'Here's your post, by the way, Mam.'

Fiona tried not to look unsettled as she examined one of them closely.

23

Buses passing the front room window marked the time. Fiona sat alone as another one roared up the hill on its way south. The pot of jasmine tea on the table in front of her had gone cold. The letter Nóra gave her, bringing both dread and elation, lay beside it.

Yes, everything changed in that summer of 1984. She could still picture the drugstore in Clarksdale where she bought the test kit, the dread as the shop owner explained the package matter-of-factly. In the hotel bathroom, she nervously removed the plastic cap to expose the absorbent tip of the stick, held it as she peed in hope, replaced the cap, and awaited her fate. Flies buzzed near her. The heat wouldn't go away. She heard a hard-sell radio ad for a burger joint somewhere offering a free cold drink. Car horns, people, a world that didn't care.

Positive. She'd never missed a period before, now it was devastation. An unwanted biological process had begun in her body. She'd keep the news to herself – she was leaving anyway – James didn't need to know. Her dad had been taken into hospital after a heart scare – she had to go back to Dublin. It shocked her how quickly the relationship had declined, how

James's attractive qualities in Dublin had melted here. Even his bubbly personality annoyed her now. Was she a bad judge of people, she wondered?

They went for beers (the drink tasted awful, the bar was grimy – or so it seemed). She tried to hide her gloom; he was all chat, where he'd go to next, how he'd manage on his own. She didn't care, disgusted at the thought of what his body – his sperm – had done to her. One evening he'd been drinking more than her. His mood got darker as the night progressed. He got very aroused back in the room, pushing her against a wall, his fingers pulling open her jeans. 'Sexy, isn't it?' he growled. Chilling still.

America became a surreal, uncomfortable host. Half-awake and half-asleep, she watched for her boarding gate and waited; New Orleans to JFK, then a stop in Shannon was the schedule. Flying into Dublin over Howth Head, the familiarity didn't bring any relief. Unconsciously she held her tummy as the plane slammed the tarmac.

Was it all a bad dream? No. The jet engines were now roaring in reverse, but for her, it wasn't possible to undo – or even slow down – the consequences of what happened late on a New York night, or maybe on the way south, she wasn't sure – and it didn't really matter anyway.

Her parents were at Arrivals, their hugs and delight at seeing her making her feel worse, her dad looking vulnerable after the heart procedure he'd had a fortnight before. On the drive home, the Dublin suburbs seemed so bleak, as she braced herself for what she was about to reveal. The comfort of being home couldn't lift her gloom; throwing down her backpack in the hallway, a lump came to her throat. 'Mum, Dad, I've something to tell you …'

'Let's have some breakfast,' her mother said nervously, looking at the table she'd laid out.

Fiona persisted. 'Mum, Dad … I'm pregnant.'

Jean let a cup drop on the floor tiles, though nobody took much notice. 'Oh, darling,' she said. Her father said nothing, just got up and walked slowly to the patio. Through the glass door Fiona saw him stand with his back to her, his hand going up to his face to wipe away tears. She felt awful.

He came back, trying to be purposeful. 'What are we going to do?'

Repetitive interrogation followed. 'Are you sure? How did this happen? Where's that James fellow? Couldn't you have been more careful? Who knows about this …?'

'Mum, Dad, I'm devastated, I'm angry, I'm sad, I don't know if I'm coming or going.'

Through her tears she noticed they were watching her rubbing her stomach in a nervous way. Back and forth Fiona's hand moved as she blubbered.

Waking from a long deep sleep hours later, she looked out the bedroom window to the garden, where her mother was bravely pruning a rosebush, the secateurs shaking in her hand. Fiona's heart went out to her. Then, she heard her dad's voice as he hurried from the house. An animated conversation followed, with hands gesturing. Fiona was happy she couldn't hear the words.

At dinner that night, the dreaded option was mentioned. 'You could go to England?' was how her dad put it. 'It's straightforward enough.'

Jean put her hands to her face and started sobbing. 'No. Not that.'

'Isn't it what thousands of Irish women do every year?' he said.

Fiona stayed silent; she didn't like the idea of abortion as a solution to unwanted pregnancy and could imagine the scene in a clinic in Manchester or London, strangers putting an end to a life. There had to be another solution.

She wandered a lot in Dublin that winter. Standing at the Daniel O'Connell monument one day, a cold east wind coming up the Liffey, she studied the symbolism: the figure of Mother Ireland, pointing up at the 'Liberator,' the 'chains of bondage' broken at her feet. That week, Fiona was sure she'd felt a tiny movement inside her – a human life maybe conscious enough to experience the Dublin cold. She felt relieved she hadn't chosen abortion. Her disquiet at the idea of termination wasn't religious at this time, though she knew her mother's abhorrence was.

'Mam,' a voice said. A Traveller woman holding a carefully swaddled baby was looking for money. 'A little help for the babby, Mam?'

Struck by the way she held the tiny baby close and her warm gaze, Fiona felt tenderness towards her.

'Are you all right, Mam?', the woman asked, like she knew why Fiona was distracted. 'I'll say a prayer for ye.'

She's going to say a prayer for *me*, Fiona thought, searching for money.

'You'll be all right, Mam. Don't worry, God has his ways.'

In the Church of St Nicholas of Myra Without, across the city, a stained-glass window by Harry Clarke represented Joseph and Mary's betrothal, reminding her vividly of that extraordinary marriage. Elderly women sat saying the rosary, quietly rolling their beads through their fingers. Behind the altar, a frieze read: 'One of the secrets of life is to make stepping-stones out of stumbling blocks.'

Fiona had important words – official language – to take in: 'As the birth mother and the child's legal guardian, your consent to the placement of the child for adoption is required.' The social worker had to be satisfied that she understood the implications, legal and personal, of the decision she was making – documents to read, forms to sign and a swearing before a Commissioner for Oaths.

All through this, Fiona convinced herself that her baby would be happy. She would go to a childless couple, bring them joy, be loved and well cared for. People in a better position than her would give her baby their very best. The *fait accompli* would keep James out of the picture.

Her mother knew the signs when the day came in April. A dash to the hospital, soothing tones from brilliant professionals, then a trolley journey, Fiona in a daze trying to manage the contractions and breathe at the same time. Doors swung open for her, the start of a well-coordinated procedure, everyone knew what they had to do. She didn't remember much of it until a small bundle was offered to her. A cry came – this little soul was claiming her place in humanity. She immediately named her Lily.

Then the trauma began: even though the circumstances of the conception still gave her nightmares, and the dread of James returning, wanting to be part of their lives was over-whelming, the love she felt for the baby tugged at her. She was in a daze – wanting to be Lily's mother but dreading the future. Could she go on – with or without her? She'd have to, the decision was made. It was the nurse's hands that fateful day she'd never forget – the decisive way they gripped the little bundle – taking possession from her.

In the weeks that followed, she was again a brooding figure on the streets, a compulsion to walk, away from home and parents, to try and make sense of it all. And she was missing her baby. Pavements seemed unyielding, the city damper than she could remember. The seagulls swooping over O'Connell bridge were crying to her, it felt. She didn't want to meet anyone she knew, wanting the city to be anonymous. But how could she pick up her life?

Walking into Trinity College one day, she met a sea of strange faces, the seat of learning clearly moving on without her. James crossed her mind uneasily as she wandered into the Buttery. A young couple were holding hands. She wanted to say, 'Be careful.'

On the way out, the statue of Oliver Goldsmith caught her eye. The sun was shining on the eighteenth-century poet. She remembered his lines:

There, in his noisy mansion, skill'd to rule,
The village master taught his little school.

That picture of harmony and order in the mythical school struck her. Thinking of becoming a teacher, the sense of satisfaction that could come from passing something on, made her feel better about herself. In the National Museum, a noisy group of kids in school uniforms were enjoying their day out. She decided on a plan – she'd go back to college study for a Higher Diploma in Education. She'd offer something to the world.

Atonement began. Her turn to faith and spirituality surprised friends but brought her a new sense of well-being. Going into a religious bookshop on North Earl Street one day, a place she wouldn't even have darkened the door of in her student days, she mixed with earnest customers looking for comfort in words. Her mother asked her about a Thomas

Merton book she'd seen in the house, *Love and Living*. Fiona marked a passage for her:

> *Love is, in fact, an intensification of life, a completeness, a fullness, a wholeness of life. We do not live merely in order to vegetate through our days until we die.*

Fiona reminded her mother about what she now saw as a 'road to Damascus' moment on their Croagh Patrick climb two years before. She volunteered for the St Vincent de Paul Society, getting to know people who'd fallen on hard times or didn't get a decent start in life in the first place. She took long walks along the seafront, often not realising how far she'd walked, several times ending up at the huge concrete Stella Maris statue at the end of the Bull Wall, built by seafarers as a tribute to Our Lady. It could be a wild spot, lashed by the sea on stormy days, yet they were the days she felt most anchored.

She lit candles in churches, imagining Lily's milestones: teething, her first words, the day she first walked. Would she be happy? Would she be told about her birth mother – what would she think of the woman who gave her away? She believed her prayers would help take care of Lily. Maybe that was her way of soothing her conscience.

Another thought: had Con, looking at the picture in her parents' house that day, spotted her bump? She'd decided not to reveal her secret way back then, changed her mind several times, worked out what she'd say, then put it off again.

Now the day she'd thought might eventually come had arrived. She read the letter again.

Dear Mrs Twomey,

I am employed with TUSLA, the Child and Family Agency. I'm contacting you to discuss a very personal and sensitive issue. I received a letter from a woman called Lillian Hopkin recently. She is in her thirties and was adopted by a family in Athlone when she was a few weeks old. She is now seeking to know the identity of her birth mother. We believe that this person is you, according to our records.

I understand that this is difficult and emotional news to hear, after so many years. So firstly, I want to assure you of my discretion and sensitivity in this matter. Birth mothers are protected by legislation. We understand that this may not be something you had been expecting. Therefore, be absolutely assured that your identity will not be revealed without your consent.

As well as the rights of adopted persons, birth parents are also protected by the laws governing the adoption process. I can tell you that you are not obliged to identify yourself or to respond to an overture by the person concerned. We are aware of the difficulties posed by this. You may be fearful of the reaction of others if they were to learn that you once placed a baby for adoption.

She put the letter down. Everything flooded back, though it had never really gone away: the relationship she regretted, the child she brought into the world now adrift from her birth family – her daughter, Lily – who wanted to know who she really was.

I appreciate that the thought of contact being established may be upsetting, as I'm sure you were told at the time that you would never see your child again.

It triggered the now-familiar imagining: what did her baby look like? Was she tall or small? Was she happy? Fiona thought of all the milestones of her first-born child she'd missed; the joys and disappointments that Lily might experience had taken place with others guiding her. Had not knowing her birth mother damaged her?

And why were they calling her Lillian? *That's a different name, I named her Lily.*

The crucial part of the letter came next.

Ms Hopkin has indicated that she would like to have direct contact with you. I suggest you give this some thought and let me know your decision in due course. Again, I must reassure you that nothing will happen further without your consent.

That part of her life was vivid again; the physicality of carrying the baby, her inner turmoil, her parents' shock. And it was still raw to remember how the subject disappeared from conversation once the adoption was finalised. Then, one day, in a darkened hospice room, her mother blurted out, 'Do you remember your little girl when you were young …?' Something was there in her mother's memory, a granddaughter she would now never know, troubling her at the end of her life.

Fiona put the letter back in the envelope and slipped it into her bag. If Lily was looking for her birth mother now, she'd want to know about her father too. Fiona shuddered at that thought; as far as she knew, James had disappeared in America, another Irish illegal. She'd decided never to contact him or his family again. She'd enough complications to deal with without him wanting a say. And there were the bitter memories of their time together.

She started composing replies in her head: *Thank you for your letter, but I have to say it came as a big shock*. Then she thought of another, tougher line: *I felt that I was being tracked down. This is a part of my life I don't want to face again. My husband and children are unaware of all this*. She thought the better of it, that was too cold. Instead, she wanted to say she'd prefer for now not to revisit this part of her past. And besides, Lily was not, apparently, in any trouble. So, she settled on the words she was happiest with: *I'm preoccupied now with a serious illness in the family*.

She paced the room, then looked out at the night, thinking of a woman somewhere, her own flesh and blood, looking for answers, maybe angry, maybe troubled in some way. There was curiosity too; the wondering and longing of years could be answered simply now – by meeting her daughter. She felt a moral duty to give something, thinking again of the concept of atonement. Better not to close any doors, so she would end the letter with: *However, please allow me time to give this more thought. I'll write to you again in a couple of months.*

It was almost dark, except for the interior lights of the buses – illuminating people going about their evening. She brought the tray with her tea things back to the kitchen. A noisy gush of water from the tap interrupted her thoughts. She washed the cups carefully and put them away. Keeping order on domestic matters was important. She went upstairs and climbed quietly into bed beside Con.

Worrying and wide awake, she imagined Lily reading a letter saying her mother – yes, that's what Fiona was – didn't want to see her, her child. Maybe Lily was just searching out of curiosity, or because she'd been to see a professional of some kind who'd suggested doing it for 'closure'?

She heard the front door open and close. It was a gentle sound, so it was Nóra; Ciarán tended to bang it. Fiona liked Nóra to be safely home before she went to sleep, protective about *this* daughter, at least. Her restlessness wouldn't go away. How would she tell them they had a half-sister? What would they think of their mother, giving up her child so easily way back then? But it hadn't been easy at all.

24

It was August 2018 and Pope Francis was in Ireland. Fiona, Con and Nóra were on the Dublin train for the big event of the visit, the World Meeting of Families Mass. Ciarán had opted out, mostly indifferent to his mother's faith. Con was reluctant, but wore his old TV hat, interested in how the spectacle would be run – the production. Nóra was sceptical but treated it like going to a festival. Only Fiona really wanted to be there. The night before, she'd watched the pope arrive at the big stadium concert, as 'Anthem' by Leonard Cohen was sung, the lines about cracks and light and human imperfection making her sob in front of the TV.

An elderly man sat opposite them. The train was halfway to Dublin when he spoke. 'I suppose you're for the Mass?'

'We are,' said Fiona.

He took out sandwiches, packed the old-fashioned way in recycled bread-wrapping paper. The train slowed down to a crawl, and he nodded at them to look out the window. 'Do you see above in that field, there's a fairy tree,' he said.

Fiona looked out and saw a solitary whitethorn bush in the middle of a field.

'Well, the farmer won't be cutting that. That's as it should be. It's for the fairies.'

The train squeaked and began to pick up speed. He slowly munched his sandwiches and didn't say another word. Nóra watched him curiously, like he was a relic of a bygone age.

Her mother looked thoughtfully at her. 'There can be other dimensions to existence, you know,' she said to her daughter. 'God, as in Dia in Irish, is not necessarily the same God of the Bible, but more to do with nature and the supernatural.'

This reflection – the glimpse of another side of her mother – covered a few kilometres of track for Nóra.

The walk to the Mass site from Heuston Station was made shorter by the high-spirited crowd, making their way through the seventeenth-century Phoenix Park. Their allotted corral wasn't too far from the stage, which had been set up in front of the giant metal cross, which marked the visit of Pope John Paul II in 1979. Even Fiona had to admit it felt already like a relic from a very different era.

She had reluctantly taken the video camera for Con. As his condition worsened, this project seemed more and more like voyeurism. But Pat had asked her to bring it. Waiting for the Pope to arrive, she gently suggested to Con he might like to record something. She watched him fiddle awkwardly with the buttons and as the camera came to life, he glowered disapprovingly at it, before walking a little from where they were sitting and looking into the lens, with a goofy expression.

'I'm here with the biggest crowd of Holy Joes you could ever meet.'

He laughed out loud.

'OK, they're really well behaved, to be sure, but … the … the … fervour all around the place is getting to me … Is this what they call "the faithful"? I'm not one of them. More a lost soul. Interesting word, that, f-a-i-t-h-f-u-l …'

Fiona caught some of what he was saying and looked at him with a startled expression. 'Put that thing away,' she said, pointing to the camera.

Con laughed. 'As the actress said to the bishop!'

'Con! Really.'

Someone beside her muttered that this was a family event. Nóra looked mortified at her Da's embarrassing joke, wondering what planet he was on.

Though rain threatened, thousands of choral voices soared, then the Pontiff appeared, his popemobile zigzagging through the crowd. The excitement grew as it passed near them, even Con got caught up in the moment, the elderly Argentinian almost obscured by flags and hands reaching out.

'It's *nearly* rock'n'roll,' Con offered, as the cheering intensified.

'Smart alec,' Fiona said, waving her yellow and white flag.

Con settled down on the grass as Mass began, dozing off during the liturgy. Pope Francis asked for forgiveness for the sins of the Church. Fiona knew that stain was part of the reason for their two-thirds empty corral. The pope alluded to, '… all those times when so many single mothers who tried to find their children that had been taken away, or those children who tried to find their mothers and were told this was a mortal sin …'

She listened without looking in Nóra's direction, the words comforting her. Her faith would bring strength with Con's illness – and as her secret was about to unfold.

After the Mass, the choir fell silent, people moved towards the exit where food vendors offloaded their surplus sandwiches. 'Ha! Look at them grabbing more than they can eat themselves. Not very, eh, Christian …?' Con said as he unwrapped one, looked at the contents and got stuck in.

At the train station, Con had a pint. Fiona opted for tea.

'Hey, fancy meeting you here!' a voice said. It was Deirdre – with Pauline. Fiona didn't hide her papal flag, happy to make her statement.

'Were you at the Mass?' she asked Pauline, winking at Deirdre.

Pauline rose to the bait. 'I wouldn't be seen dead at it.'

'I'd say you were at the counterdemonstration,' said Con. 'Was Hozier any good?'

'"Take Me to Church", I bet he sang it?' Fiona chipped in.

'Wow, I like that song,' Nóra said. She teased her mother. 'How did I end up at the wrong gig?'

Fiona was relieved when the call came for the Galway train; she regarded Pauline as a person who seemed angry and snarky, as if waiting to be offended. They said their goodbyes. Con looked at the two as they walked away. 'What's a woman like Pauline doing wearing Doc Martens?'

'Cop on, Dad!' Nóra said, lifting her foot to show her red Docs, like she wanted to give him a boot. 'Look!'

On the train, Con was soon asleep, his head leaning against Fiona as evening fell on the midlands. At the series of Victorian-era stations, weary passengers disembarked into the night. The engine revs, the lonesome-sounding whistles before leaving each station made Fiona wonder why rail travel felt so nostalgic.

Outside Kent Station in Cork, she saw Nóra say hello to a young lad and felt a sudden protective pang at what her daughter was facing in her life: choices, relationships, vulnerability. She smiled at him – but not her business really.

Nóra made tea when they got in and summed up the day for Ciarán. 'It was a bit holy, but I'm glad I went. Mam was still holding her papal flag when we reached Cork. Oh, and Dad slept a lot.'

Fiona was soon alone, Con asleep, the house quiet. The pope's words about mothers and babies came back. She thought of Lily; had she been at the Mass, or watching on TV, at an alternative event, or maybe she didn't care at all?

A bass thump-thump-thump came from next door as she slipped into bed. They were partying late. Raucous laughter made it through the wall. But more than that was keeping her awake. She remembered the failed attempt to talk to Con on the holiday. How could she possibly explain Lily and that whole story now?

25

ike wheels ticked; pedals creaked. Nóra and her friend,
Iseult were heading off on an evening spin. It was the
spring of 2019. Girl talk and laughs might make Nóra
forget her dad was still a missing person. The season was so
appealing – trees flushed with green, gardens coming to life,
everyone happier in themselves.

Down the street, a group of lads sat boisterously on a wall.
The girls slowed down, exchanging knowing glances. The one
who'd caught Nóra's eye before was among them, long locks
waving as he messed with the others, tall and graceful for a
bloke – yes, attractive. Since the day at the station, she'd wished
something would happen between them, but not being confident or pushy, a move would have to come from him. Each of
them waved. Her heart pounded – but she didn't give anything
away.

Their route took them down the greenway by the harbour,
towards Blackrock. The light was holding so they headed
south, the chat propelling them along. They passed sweating
power walkers, now out in force on the nice evening.

'Any news of your dad?' Iseult asked, lowering her voice.

'No. It's four days now, but it seems a lot longer. Still no leads. Mam is in bits.'

She looked away to the water, remembering the walks here with him years before – in her troubled time. She came to like the ritual of getting ready to go out, donning coat and boots. After they'd tramped well out of the city, they'd sit and eat the sandwiches her mother made. In time, she realised his intention wasn't to directly confront her eating issue, but to show her positivity, the constancy and wonder of the world around her. He'd wave his hands animatedly, encouraging her to believe problems could be overcome, though they appear insurmountable. Astronomy featured; staring up at the sky, he told her about Aristotle's belief that because the shadow cast by the earth on the moon was always curved, therefore the earth had to be round.

'No computers, no telescope, naked eye only. Amazing, wasn't it?'

'Yes, Dad.'

They braved the steady drizzle and a biting wind to walk part of the old Cork to Crosshaven railway line, listening to each other's footsteps, neither speaking, just thinking.

'Patrick Kavanagh called it the "oriental streets of thought", you know?' Con said, breaking the silence.

He told her the modern-day parable about the drunk man who drops his keys. 'He'll never find them if he only looks where the streetlights are shining.'

Something had sunk in during those afternoons. She looked at the darkening sky and sure enough, the moon had a small, curved shadow on it.

If only she could help *him* now.

She stopped pedalling. Up ahead, a man stared in their direction. The girls exchanged glances. You never knew who you'd meet down this way. As they drew closer to the tall, bearded man, Nóra was startled to recognise the ragged-looking figure.

'Dad ...?'

26

Con stood looking around the kitchen like a stranger might, as if he didn't live there and didn't recognise the order of the scene in front of him. Cupboards, delph, pottery pieces and appliances were all in place. Fiona always ran the house well, but the tidiness, the ordered world, felt alien now. Scratching his head absently, he tried to think why he was about to go out. Work? No, that was all over, mornings he'd be out the door, all business-like, by 8.30?

There hadn't been much interrogation from the family about his missing days, most of which he didn't remember – except the chill of cold nights. Meeting Nóra that evening made something in his brain click; sentiment or nostalgia kicked in, and he passively took part in the joy and relief of the homecoming. The visits from the garda, a social worker, the curious neighbours, all passed him by. He had no sense, either, of the awkward movements he'd acquired or the deterioration in his personal hygiene.

Today, Nóra was minding him. Fiona had left earlier that morning to drive to Athlone, to meet an old friend there, she said. *What was that about?*

The sun streaming through the windows encouraged Con to get going. First, he'd a problem to deal with: he was supposed to feed the cat but couldn't remember if he'd done it already. The task confused him. The tabby seemed contented and ignored him. Better play it safe and feed her again. He and the cat had history. So, what did she eat? Yes, food from a bag kept under the sink.

Fiona had left him a flask of tea. He sat down to pour but the relationship between flask, liquid and cup puzzled him. Opening the newspaper, he idly flicked pages till an analysis of Manchester United's fortunes caught his eye. He tried some cereal, but it just didn't taste right. It looked like oats and wheat and raisins, but it didn't taste like it should. A happy cat purred at his feet.

'Nóra! Are you getting up?'

He hadn't made much headway with the newspaper, none the wiser about Man U, despite starting the article several times. He considered a shower and a shave but let the opportunity pass.

Nóra came into the room and noticed her mother had left a picture of Con's father on the table. 'Wasn't that sweet of Mam?' she said. 'She knew it was grandad's anniversary.'

Con hadn't noticed, but now he looked intently at it. His heard his dad say, 'Listen to this, boi,' as a needle crackled and up came the jangling piano intro to 'Like A Rolling Stone.' Where was Da now? Maybe he could call to the house and find them both waiting there. He wiped tears clumsily with his sleeve.

'Are you OK, Dad?'

'What are we doing now?' he asked her.

'We're going for a walk, Dad.'

They headed off down the street, arm in arm.

'You know where you are, don't you?' she asked as they passed places now only vaguely familiar to him, The South Mall, The Crawford Gallery, The Opera House. It was the route he took to work, an age ago it seemed. Crossing Christy Ring Bridge, they looked down on the water.

'You used to talk a lot about the river, remember? You used to ask us how many tributaries we could name?' Nóra nudged gently.

Con couldn't look anymore.

A man came towards them. 'Howya, boi' he said. 'It's well you're looking!'

Con tried to register this man's identity. He was about his own age, carrying a briefcase that looked vaguely familiar.

'I'm Pat, Con, don't you remember me?' the man said, glancing at Nóra and trying to sound normal.

Con's face contorted, like he was in pain. Struggling to get the words out, he managed, 'Not so bad,' more a reflex than a real reply. Then he remembered. 'Pat ... sorry.' He stared at a car as it passed them. 'How's ... business going?'

Pat was clearly relieved at the normal question. 'Well, wait till I tell you. Didn't I get a ten-part nature series with –'

Con interrupted. 'Pat!' he said again. A rush of recollection had come – cameras, editing suites, contracts, faces around a table, arguments, once the stuff of a normal week.

'Con, wait till I tell you.' Pat was all enthusiasm now. 'Didn't someone find the camera you dropped into the river last month?'

'Camera …?'

Pat said the bag had stayed afloat long enough for a curious kayaker to pull it out of the water. The company name was on a plate on the bag. After careful drying, the memory card's contents were found to have survived.

'I've been going through the footage, boi. Not bad material,' he said, guiltily. 'You're like a Shakespearian character in it with those little soliloquies.'

Nóra thought she'd better take the situation in hand. Her dad should have enjoyed meeting an old colleague, but he didn't seem to. 'We'd better keep moving, Dad.'

'All the best, Con. Bye, Nóra. Mind your dad,' said Pat, turning to go.

Con's mind had already moved on: Shakespeare had him back in his old school classroom this time. They were doing *King Lear*. Fear had made him learn the lines then. Now they were vivid. He was nervously reciting; a stumble could mean a smack. The room and the desks were in front of him. There was a musty smell, of clothes, chalk, the remains of lunches. A faded map of the world on the wall invited dreams of not being in this place. The schoolroom lines kept flowing.

Does any here know me? Why, this is not Lear.
Does Lear walk thus, speak thus? Where are his eyes?

'Well done, Twomey. You got there.' The teacher was stern, but not cruel. Con wasn't one of the swaggering kids in the class. He kept to himself a bit. The teacher's voice kept booming, its echo got longer, then started to fade. Con didn't want to be back in that classroom; one or two boys were giving him a hard time. He saw the map again; where did he dream of going? That vast space called USSR looked forbidding; and they don't have food to eat a lot of the time, the teacher told them. Scandinavia, maybe, a cold but mysterious place; women there had a reputation for being racy, they weren't hung up about sex, one of the lads once claimed, though how he knew this was a mystery.

'Scandinavia … Denmark …' he said aloud, turning to his daughter.

'What's that, Dad?'

'Oh. Nothing.'

Turning right into Coburg Street, a weather-beaten looking man shouted from across the street.

'Hey! Con, is it?'

They stared at a grubby man, sitting on a sheet of cardboard waving a can of cheap beer, like he was toasting Con.

'Ye don't recognise your old friends now, do ye, boi, with your nice girlfriend there?' he said, wheezing and coughing.

Con looked across at the man. Nóra didn't ask questions.

They were outside the Corner House, and she changed the subject. 'You always really liked this place, Dad.'

He tried to recall how fond he was of the pub, and great nights in it. "Sean nós singing meeting America, fiddles and banjos letting rip freely in different codes," he'd once written about the place. He looked at the door.

'Mind that fella, young one. He can fairly put away drink when he wants to,' the man said, shuffling off.

'Dad, you go in. I need to go down to Patrick Street to pick something up. I'll see you in a little while.' Con nodded and pushed the door.

'How are things, Con?' the woman behind the bar greeted him.

He hesitated. 'Ah … ye know!' Then a pause and a frown. She changed the subject: 'You missed some great music here the other night.' Half looking away, he felt negative. 'Fellas who still think it's the sixties or seventies, but it's not.'

She tried to change the subject. 'How are the family?'

Con had to think about it. 'Ciarán has finished College. Nóra is …'

He couldn't remember what third-level course it was.

The woman saw the difficulty. 'They're thriving, anyway? Good.'

He stared at the tap dispensing one of his favourite drinks, malty-tasting Lon Dubh stout, but opted for a coffee instead. There was only one other customer in the bar, a man sitting contentedly, a pint in front of him. Con envied his ease with the world, the contentment of a quiet drink with no cares. Trying to avoid any more questions, he took his coffee and sat down at a table.

He could hear Ralph Vaughan Williams's 'The Lark Ascending' coming from a radio behind the bar. He liked the invocation of nature, a sweet tone from the solo violin filled the pub.

'Ah, I'll go a pint of the Lon Dubh,' he said, tiring of the coffee.

He looked around him, deciding to address the man at the bar. 'Have you any secrets?'

The man looked startled. Con raised his voice. 'Ha! You can tell me. I'll have forgotten by the time I leave here.'

The woman serving looked his way but decided to leave well enough alone. She knew people were wary of him; he might say something strange, aggressive even. A minute later he seemed serene, sitting by the fire with his pint. But he wasn't. He was thinking about Athlone.

As the music finished, thoughts were queuing up in his head that he couldn't make sense of; first, another lark altogether – the Cork one in Ger Wolfe's song.

You were the lark of Mayfield
Tumbling down the hill …

And he remembered the lark a day on a bog somewhere, with Fiona. *When was it? A few summers ago?*

Nóra arrived back, glad to see he was still there. 'Did you enjoy the pint, Dad?'

But Con was disturbed.

'What was your mother doing in Athlone?'

'I dunno. Meeting an old school friend, or something. Anyway, we should head home.'

She waited till he stood up and led him towards the door.

He furrowed his brow. 'I don't like the sound of *that*,' he said, spitting the words out.

27

Fiona manoeuvred the car into a space, her stomach rumbling again. Her foot slipped off the clutch before she turned off the engine, and the car lurched forward, prompting an anxious glance from another car. She was trying to control her nerves. Over several months, she'd been through a delicate process of consultation – begun with a letter saying she was ready for the meeting.

The venue arranged was a café in the town called The Left Bank, on the far side of the Shannon. She'd researched where it was and how to get there so there'd be no hiccups. Still, her nerves had her confused at the river. It was flowing south, so the left bank (and the café, too) should be behind her on the east side, the address she was looking for was across the river, the right bank, as the river flows. Had Paris got it the wrong way around?

Watching the swirls and eddies, she remembered the Aubrey de Vere poem she'd learned in school, 'The Ballad of Athlone', celebrating the deeds of the Jacobite forces here in 1691, men dying in an attempt to dismantle a bridge to halt the Williamite advance.

> *Oh, who for Erin will strike a stroke*
> *Who'll hurl you planks where the waters roar?*

This kind of thing wasn't celebrated in schoolrooms nowadays. The sky was a darkening grey now, different shades of it reflected in the water, timelessly. As the poem had it:

> *The Shannon swept onwards broad and clear …*

Walking on, her jitters eased. An imposing curved wall of stone, the twelfth-century Athlone Castle loomed like it was sitting in judgement, Fiona continued down Main Street, the colours of the buildings contrasting with the castle's solemn stone. Passing Seán's Bar, a sign proclaimed it Ireland's oldest pub. A few metres further on, she nervously opened the café door. The tasteful interior was welcoming, as was the aroma of coffee and cooking.

Across the wooden floor, a woman shifted uneasily at a table. Dark-haired and in her mid-thirties, it had to be her. The likeness was scary, as if Fiona was looking at herself in a mirror some thirty years earlier. The giant hands of a clock were spinning uncontrollably backwards in her head, like they used to do in films. Her eyes and the other woman's – identical shades of blue, the magic of Nature – met. As she walked across the room, she put a hand on a chair to steady herself.

The first word came hesitantly. 'Lily?'

'Lillian, yes.' Fiona was being corrected.

A self-consciousness suddenly overcame her. Hospital smells from long ago were back, nurses fussing, the last time since she'd seen this mature adult was as a tiny baby. She smoothed the lapels of her coat that were already fine. Her body felt rigid as her long-lost little girl stood up and came towards her.

'Hi … Mum.'

They hugged, sniffling, tears came in unison, then they drew back smiling as they noticed each other's makeup running. After the tactile moment, Fiona began assessing her child's shape, complexion, sense of dress, her voice.

'Let's sit down,' she said.

The unspooling of lives began, like pages of an old book turning over slowly. Lily was married to a scientist who worked for a multinational pharmaceutical firm based on the outskirts of town. Her own job, as a history and geography teacher, was in the town, and she'd finished for the day.

'How was your journey?' she asked.

'Fine,' said Fiona, anxious to get the small talk over, wanting to dive straight in. Their situation felt surreal. 'I'm sorry this all took so long,' she offered. 'My life was in turmoil, with Con … you know, my husband, he's ill.'

'I'm sorry,' Lily said, sounding matter of fact, perfunctory about a character in a drama she'd been written out of. Lily seemed to search Fiona's face before the simple question: 'Did you ever think about me over the years?'

'I did. All the time.'

They looked at each other for several seconds. Fiona adjusted her chair, noisily scraping the wooden floor, and brushed back her hair before she answered. 'I resolved that I didn't want to cause confusion or uncertainty, I would let you have as normal a life as possible with your family – your new family, that is.'

Lily was silent, before a voice eased the tension: 'Would you like to see the menu?'

Both glanced nervously at the options and ordered quickly, hardly looking at the menu at all. Lily paused, taking a sip of water.

'Did you ever worry that I might not be happy?' Another of the difficult questions Fiona had anticipated.

'I did, but I suppressed it. I … I used to go to my local church, say a prayer and light a candle for you. You were always in my thoughts and in my heart.'

Lily put down her glass of water. 'A candle?' she said. 'You believe in that stuff?'

Fiona was taken back at the way Lily's mouth curled, dismissively.

'I do,' she said, thinking of all the reflective moments she'd spent alone in cavernous churches, watching the small wick in countless candles flicker to life, her pain for her daughter, the belief she was empowering some spirit, that protection for her little girl could come from this small ritual. Would her baby get through adolescence, deal with exams, the pressures – taunts – from other kids? Now, that subject of all her prayers seemed a rather over-confident woman who looked sceptically at her.

'The hypocrisy that goes with religion and piety has done so much damage to this country,' Lily proclaimed.

Fiona understood that Lily might be angry. She was tempted to say that but for her views on abortion decades before, they mightn't be sitting here now. She decided against.

'I didn't mean to offend,' Lily said, moving her hand towards Fiona in a gesture of comfort. Silence, and both glanced around them.

'I thought about you, too, once I had been told that I was adopted. My parents were open with me about everything else, but I wasn't told the truth until I was going to college. I didn't know whether to imagine my birth mother as a girl who didn't want to be inconvenienced by a child, or a vulnerable woman exploited by some man.'

Fiona had to think about that. 'It was neither, I think.'

She thought a thousand times about how she might answer questions like this, especially on the drive here. She pictured herself as a twenty-two-year-old, all of thirty-five years before.

'I agonised, I walked the streets, I talked to my parents, and, in the end, I thought it best that you would have a mother and father rather than just a mother. I had no certainty in my life at the time.'

'If you'd kept me, would your parents have supported you?'

'Yes, I think they would.' Fiona said, her head down, examining the tablecloth's pattern with a finger.

'So, tell me about my dad.'

Fiona looked up slowly. 'We got together in Trinity – we were in the same year. Your father was this good-looking fella, dashing, mischievous. We were mad about each other at the beginning, but our relationship burnt out, I'm afraid. One of the things that drew me was his passion for American music – it was edgy and exciting. We ended up in the States the summer you were (she hesitated on the word) … conceived.'

She sighed. 'We were kids, basically.'

'This looks nice,' Fiona said as lunch arrived, trying to sound relaxed, though she didn't lift her knife and fork to the quiche. She was trying to compose her thoughts, something that was proving difficult. Explanations about a birth control mishap, youthful carelessness, dislike of abortion, all competed in her head. That summer wasn't pleasant to recall, but she had to.

'The dusty Delta sounds romantic, but romance can evaporate too – go very sour. I suppose America was a test for us and we came unstuck that first summer.'

Lily just picked at her food as Fiona continued.

'We split up; I went back to Dublin, and he disappeared into America. Driven by his interest, we'd done Memphis, then Muddy Waters' birthplace and the Crossroads in Clarksdale. He was all talk about Chicago Blues, so he probably headed north. I don't know where he ended up.'

Lily wanted more. 'Have you any photos from that time?'

'No, I'm afraid not. Just memories.'

More were floating back; half-rusted rail tracks that disappeared towards the horizon, tufts of weeds growing up between them; shacks, oceans of crops and the sticky, muggy air. Fiona thought of the juke joint they found; James, excited as a child, but his obsession wearing thin for her already – 'Wouldn't that groove make your bones vibrate?' But romance had left her heart. She was stuck with a man with a darker side – moodiness and aggression – who took it out on her.

She paused the internal playback.

'At least we were adventurous, weren't we?'

'What was my father's surname?'

Fiona knew she couldn't avoid that question. She paused, thinking of the implications.

'Forsythe,' she said, with a tremor in her voice.

'I have a big interest in American history,' Lily said. 'I did a master's degree on the Irish emigrants in Pennsylvania in the nineteenth century, the peasants who became proletarianized. Really interesting.'

She'd lived and worked in Pittsburgh as part of her research. 'It's where I met my husband. Pete is his name.'

Irish emigrants kept their language, she explained. Some turned to crime and produced the Molly Maguires. Fiona was struck by one of the stories: how the sky blackened, like an eclipse, in Glenfinn in Donegal, at the moment in 1877 when an emigrant from there was hanged three thousand miles away. 'He'd written home asking them to pray for him,' Lily said, seeing Fiona liked the story.

Lily was curious about the journey through Robert Johnson country. 'Of course, there was another side to the Johnson legend,' she said. 'Women would dread him arriving in their town, because it meant an excuse for drunkenness by the menfolk. Johnson looked for women to use as he needed them. He left a trail behind him, of drunken men and broken-hearted women.'

Fiona couldn't resist. 'Your father embraced some of that spirit.'

She changed the subject; there were things about Lily's life she wanted to know. 'How ... how are your ... *adoptive* parents?' she said, self-consciously stumbling on the word.

'They're fine. Brendan and Marion. They – we – have a shoe shop in town, though it's only ticking over now; they're semi-retired. The bell rings when the door opens – that kind of place. We lived over the shop, came and went to our home through it. I know the smell of leather and polish like few others. And have you noticed my midlands drawl?'

Fiona imagined life in the rooms above the shoe shop, Lily as a child. She made a timeline calculation: Lily was 11 when Fiona married Con, became a teenager the year Ciarán was born. Lives in parallel, not that far from each other.

'My adoptive parents, they did their best,' Lily offered.

'You got to college, didn't you?' Fiona said gently.

'Yes, in Galway. It was a sacrifice for them. They told me I was adopted the year I started. College was exciting and it nearly took my mind off it. I don't know why they waited, it would all have come out anyway when I applied for a passport.'

She paused, put her knife and fork down, though she'd hardly eaten anything. 'I started using their first names after that.'

Fiona watched her wince, trying not to betray anything. 'My husband tells me I should see more of them.'

Fiona imagined a kindly woman in the twilight of a hard-working life, a man liking his couple of pints in an old pub somewhere in the town, both proud of their daughter, proud of her achievements.

'Would it have been better not to have known about your birth mother?' Fiona ventured.

'Truth matters,' Lily said.

Fiona had reservations about increasing the rights of adopted people to trace their birth parents. Didn't biological parents have rights, too? Looking at this beautiful young woman sitting in front of her, she understood more. Adults made choices, like she and James did, but children had no choice about the circumstances of their conception, about being born. They grow up wanting to know who they are, wanting to know they are loved and to be reassured about their place in the world. Hadn't they a right to know that too?

Lily shifted in her chair. 'Tell me about *your* life?'

It wasn't as easy to answer as it might seem, those years after her breakup with James, her baby's birth and the aftermath, her life since. She gave a matter-of-fact account of her family and twenty-five years of marriage, about Lily's half-sister and -brother, living in Cork, her teaching career. She decided to go easy on the detail – a guilty feeling nagged at her. Yet, she didn't have to worry about sounding too contented when she came to her life now with Con.

After a couple of hours, and several coffees, Lily looked restless and stood up from the table. 'I'm sorry but I really have to go now.'

Fiona thought her daughter's expression said, 'About thirty-five years ago you handed me, a tiny baby, over to my fate, and walked away …' But Lily didn't say that. They hugged each other, warmly. Fiona noticed a mirror on the wall. 'Look,' she said, manoeuvring to pose cheek to cheek in front of it. It was a peculiar moment; two faces together in joy or sadness, she wasn't sure. She wanted to read Lily's eyes, fascinated again by the likeness. A selfie opportunity presented itself, but neither reached for their phones and the moment passed.

Deep in thought she crossed the bridge again, absently recalling the Shannon's statistics: a gradient of 1 in 15, 000, it drops only 15 metres in 200 kilometres, the river distracting her from thoughts of Lily and the meeting. Looking at the sky, Carl Sagan's 'little blue dot' came to mind, the distant image of our world demonstrating the folly of human conceits. What to make of it all, she wasn't sure?

It took her a while to find where she'd parked. Everything felt like a big task: finding the key, the door a little stiff, several attempts to start the engine. Traffic out of the town was bumper-to-bumper evening traffic. A drastic thought came: *That's my daughter, but I'm not sure I like her.* She'd been offered counselling before the meeting, but she thought she'd be OK and declined. Now she wasn't sure.

Ferbane, Birr, Roscrea, Templemore, she negotiated the towns as if on autopilot, relieved every time a traffic light glowed green for her in the twilight. Between Thurles and the M8 that would take her efficiently to the outskirts of Cork, she stopped for petrol. As a wind blew across the functional forecourt, she checked her phone as the pump hummed. There was a text message. *It was good to meet you. I hope we can meet again soon. Safe journey, Mum!*

Lillian. A mix of emotions spun in her head, like a lottery's wheel – surprise, pleasure, annoyance, guilt. Which would the pointer land on? It clicked on a smile. Had she read the meeting wrong? It was her daughter, after all. A first meeting this time, but unfinished business from the past would have to be dealt with when they met again.

As she drove on, she thought about the memoir she was working on – a new scene came to her.

It was his body – the flesh and blood that had once aroused so much, the touches that had brought ecstasy. Now it meant sweat, odour, awkwardness, a threatening presence, sex as ugliness. In the dingy room I felt trapped. If I could only be away – in a wilderness beyond the town – among the clamour of birds, instead of in this bed with this man.

I heard malevolent rumbles in the distance, longed for the crack of thunder, the downpour that might cleanse.

It was dusk when she joined the motorway. She always enjoyed the view of the Galtee Mountains to the right and the Knockmealdowns to the left from this otherwise functional road, imagining hiking on the slopes or getting lost in the valleys, the way she felt. Just dark shapes now, they chimed with her feelings. The road home was clear, and her gloom began to life the more she thought about Lily's text.

An old Toyota with a back light missing sat in front of her on the road going very slowly. Overtaking it, she caught a glimpse of the elderly couple inside, the man crouched over the wheel driving with great focus, but happy to take their time. What was Fiona's anguish about, she wondered, as the little car receded in her mirror; there's contentment to be had at all stages of life.

Aware of a heated discussion on the radio, she didn't turn it up, though the exchange sounded increasingly angry. Thoughts of a man, who might be alive or dead, possibly somewhere in North America, tumbled in. What would he be like now and how had life treated him? And a young woman had returned to suburban Athlone looking drained; what would her husband make of her account of the last few hours?

But a man was walking the streets of Cork at that moment, a rage building in his damaged brain.

28

A sudden breeze made the window blind flap, startling Fiona as she lay awake. It felt ghostly. Her mind was in overdrive. She caught sight of a framed photo on the wall. Con in his student days, smiling at the camera, a teenage U2 on the stage behind him, in the Arcadia Ballroom, full of youthful vigour – like the band, looking ready to conquer the world. Now there was a different person in the bed beside her. She thought she was getting used to him being home again, dealing with the silences, the neediness, the disappearing whiskey bottles, vague recollections of the lost days – but she wasn't *really*. He was breathing softly now, but Con awake was a different story; strange moods, scowls, contorting his face for no apparent reason. Living with a stranger was frightening.

She'd been reading again about the disease and when it might start in the brain. Research made her feel proactive. Tentatively, she'd started a discussion with him earlier that evening: 'Con, do you remember that day a few years ago when we went to Belfast?'

'Eh, kind of …'

She was nervous about continuing, such was his mood – but went on.

Connolly Station Dublin, the summer of 1993. A mill of people, whistles blowing, a departure board offering the promise of different destinations, trains getting ready to pull out. They met at the entrance to the concourse, where Fiona showed him the building's Italianate façade. 'Imposing architecture was a way of inspiring confidence in the new technology of train travel, back in the early nineteenth century,' she said, surveying the scene around them, watching vapour from a departing train rise towards the tarnished iron and glass roof.

Now, Con sat motionless as Fiona continued. 'It was your plan for a day out. Remember?'

They were going to search out places that inspired Van Morrison as a teenager. She was enthusiastic – mainly because Con was.

'You're thinking?' he said, as they sat contented with coffees in the station's exotically named Oslo bar.

'Yes …' she said. 'I'm thinking about … how happy I am.'

At that time, she'd contemplated revealing her secret. Keeping it troubled her. She decided again not to risk it – there'd be a *right* time – someday.

As their train left Dublin, a man and woman sat down opposite them. The four exchanged glances.

'You got nosey then, didn't you, Con?'

He'd watched the woman open a magazine crossword on the table in front of them, but failed to make much headway, her pen poised in her hand. He leaned across to see the clues. 'Ah, two down, an alcoholic drink made from honey, four letters, do you see that one?' he said in a stage whisper.

She looked suspiciously at him.

'Mead,' he said.

'How do you spell that?' She was enthusiastic now.

He leaned across again. 'Do you see that one, four across, five letters, the fruit of an oak tree, first letter "A?"'

The man eyed Con.

'It's acorn,' Con said.

Fiona was struck by the forwardness. Let the woman do her own crossword.

The man spoke. 'How can you be readin' with the page the other way around?' he asked, as a voice called, 'Tickets, please!'

'Where are you heading?' Con continued.

'We're going to visit my father's grave,' said the woman.

They'd left Wexford that morning early, changed trains in Dublin, and would change again at Belfast Central.

'I really loved my father; he was a powerful man and I miss him every day.'

Con recognised the distinctive accent, Irish but not of a particular region.

'It's important for me to make this visit,' she continued.

Fiona knew Travellers believed more than others that death does not mark the end. The spirit lives on and the graveside is a special place to continue grieving and show respect for the dead.

'I'll be able to talk to him there,' she said. 'Margaret's my name. He's Francie.'

Con sighed as Fiona continued: 'Do you remember what you asked Francie next? You asked him was he a Traveller. I thought that was cheeky.'

Con saw the studs on Francie's ears, the heavy rings on several fingers, and knew the accent. He had always been fascinated by Traveller culture. There was a pause.

'What if I am?' Francie had said.

Fiona nudged Con's leg.

Nobody said anything for a while after that, letting the train rattle and sway.

Fiona wondered now had something started happening in Con's brain way back then, recalling something she'd read about Alzheimer's. It causes impairment of social cognition, the cognitive ability to process information coming from others – like emotions. *But that far back?* (She knew now that the night they were having dinner and he got upset about the painting could be explained by the disease).

Con wasn't paying attention, but she continued. 'Francie kept throwing dark stares in your direction.'

Clearing Dundalk, Slieve Gullion came into view before the first cross border stop at Newry. A lone Union flag defiantly fluttering in a housing estate reminded passengers they were now in the United Kingdom. Before long, Divis Mountain was on their left. West Belfast sprawled out beneath it. Recent history was difficult and hadn't been kind to this city – the good, the bad, the cruel.

At Belfast Central, they said goodbye as Margaret and Francie headed for their connection.

Fiona admired their loyalty to tradition. 'They're on their own pilgrimage. There's something in strong faith, isn't there?'

'What about ye?' the taxi driver barked before the black taxi tracked around famous icons, the Samson and Goliath cranes, heading towards Van country.

'You were pushing your journo instincts a bit there with Francie?' Fiona said. 'He nearly took a swing at you!'

Con just hummed to himself, peering at street signs, pointing out landmarks. On a narrow street of terraced houses, they stopped outside number 125.

'This is the cradle of one of the twentieth century's music greats,' he declared.

The fervour fascinated Fiona. Con couldn't stop. 'Wondrous things came out of this humble street, that house. Doesn't Van's music prove there was always another Belfast, an un-bitter place, where people sang, and read books, had fun, like in other places?' he said.

Fiona paraphrased a song she'd heard. 'Something just got mislaid, but not lost?'

Later, they bagged a comfy snug in the Crown Bar, its Baroque interior and stained-glass panels creating an intimate atmosphere for them. They drank and talked and talked, barely noticing the pub beginning to fill up with after-work people. They were very close now to each other.

'It's great to be in a new city with you,' she said.

The privacy of the snug allowed them to kiss. Forgetting about the time, they needed to run to catch the last train to Dublin.

Then she remembered him saying, on one of the east Belfast streets, as he reflected on song writing, 'Isn't memory so impressive? You can turn it on and off, summon things, recall words, get nostalgic. You can control it, too, order different thoughts and images. It's such a powerful tool; imagine if a song was in your head, but you couldn't remember the lyrics; or talk to someone and not remember what they said.'

No such reflections now from Con; he was nodding off again. Fiona looked around the room, saw the un-played guitar and bookshelves of well-read music biographies. Where was all that information now? Her eye also caught the collection of Scandinavian writers, plays by Ibsen and Strindberg, a relatively recent interest that he never explained.

Con's snoring stopped suddenly. His hands clutched the armrests, a startled look on his face.

Fiona raised her voice. 'I was going back twenty-five years, describing pictures for you, and you just slept through it.

'I didn't really,' he said.

She saw her husband, handsome, lovable – big physique, a winning smile, a lovely turn of phrase, a tender touch despite everything. Then he held his arms out for a hug.

'Fiona, that was so sweet, I love the way you told the story.'
She was sure he hadn't been paying attention.

'Oh, darling,' she said.

Suddenly, he took his arms away. She felt them go limp but said nothing.

She was getting him ready to take another shower before bed, the grime from his weeks on the street not quite gone. Fiona began with the usual instruction about taking off his clothes.

'What should I take off?'

'Everything.'

'Everything?'

'Yes.'

He stepped into the shower. She helped him turn on the water. It was messy; the relationship between the roles of soap and water had become too complicated for him. He put the bar of soap to his mouth, let water spray everywhere. The simple task of washing defeated him, and he was now in terrible form.

'Athlone ...' she thought she heard him mumble, while attempting to dry himself. Turning around to reach for something on a shelf, Fiona felt a forceful blow to the back of her head followed by stinging pain. She thought her feet left the ground; such was the force. She screamed out in pain and shock, stumbling forward but managing to put her hands out to steady herself against a cupboard. Seconds passed before she realised what had happened, though it felt much longer. The force of the fist made her bite her tongue, her blood flowing in her mouth. Light-headed and stunned, she felt herself falling into a faint and tried steady herself. Con seemed oblivious to his violence. Reeling and afraid of losing consciousness she called out to him, hoping he'd realise what he'd just done and help her.

'What's wrong with you?' he growled.

She'd never seen him look so angry, his features distorted and terrifying.

'You … hit me.'

'No, I didn't.'

He looked innocently at her. Shaking, sore and a bit woozy, she stumbled forward through the door on to the landing, and propped herself against the wall, his violence sinking in, her head feeling like it had been knocked out of place. Around her, the house had become a strange place.

Ignoring her, Con shuffled towards their bedroom. As he passed the row of banisters, she thought, half dreaming, of the day he'd painstakingly sanded and painted them, singing to himself, and looking for praise for his handiwork. The bedroom door closed behind the man who never laid a hand on anyone, who would chastise her if she administered a little smack to one of the kids.

'Oh, Mam, that's awful. But it's not Dad's fault, it's the disease,' Nóra said as she examined the wound, her mother sipping tea in silence.

Fiona lay awake for a long time in the spare room, thoughts out of control in the darkness. Could she ever share a bed with Con again? In the end, she tiptoed to their room and crept quietly into bed beside him, lying on her side and carefully placing her head on to the pillow. Touching the sore and swollen bump, she would lie this way and not move. He looked peaceful as he slept, the benign expression had returned. It surprised her that she still wanted to feel tenderly towards him as her head ached. But she knew Ciarán was right when he suggested it was time for the people with the white coats.

29

In the reception area of St Malachy's home, men sat silently with family members, or just gazed out to the grounds. But Fiona had to go where the patients were supervised. A month had passed, and Con's life was lived now behind a security door. Approaching the desk, she unconsciously rubbed the back of her neck. The bruise was gone, but not the memory of that night, or the lingering pain in her head.

When she took the pen to sign the visitor's log, she saw a strange name beside his. Con didn't get many visitors.

'Has someone come to see Con?', she asked, surprised.

The receptionist was matter-of-fact. 'Yes,' she said. 'She's come a long way.' It felt like a rebuke.

The 'she' caused a little tremble. She looked again at the name: Kirsten Frifelt. Who was she? Trying not to be startled, she just signed in the space provided, as she always did.

She walked to the ward and rang the bell. Behind the glass door, two patients shuffled by, but it was no use trying to catch their attention; they were long past being able to press buttons. A nurse Fiona knew came and the door clicked.

'Hi, Jessa,' she said. 'How is Con?'

'The same,' she said softly. They appreciated each other. Jessa never gave up trying to communicate with him.

'He has a visitor,' she smiled.

On the corridor, Fiona noticed again a former patient's self-portrait, the face with a vacant, primitive expression, the eyes the remarkable part – no detail, just white spaces. Had the artist forgotten to colour them, or was it just the way he wanted to portray his own state? Was someone trying to explain their altered self? The painting demonstrated application, talent, but ultimately, despair. It was hard not to feel down passing it. Further on, a framed poster listed the presidents of Ireland one by one, with their years in office, the staff's forlorn efforts at pedagogy. It was almost like being in a junior school, not a place of woe for unfortunates at the other end of their lives.

Approaching Room 6 she heard a woman's voice, singing in an unfamiliar language. It stopped as Fiona entered. A tall woman looked around. *Who is she?* The woman had long blonde hair, her eyes a vivid blue, but a steely look – as far as Fiona was concerned. An awkward silence followed.

'My name is Kirsten. I hope you don't mind … singing is good therapy.'

Fiona was curious about the accent. She decided to assert herself. 'I don't think we've met before.'

'I'm a friend of Con's, from the TV business,' was the answer. 'I think he has been liking Ibsen's work, and the song is tender.'

'I don't know it,' Fiona said.

It is 'Solveig's Song', from *Peer Gynt*,' Kirsten said. 'In English it would be "if you wait above, we'll meet there again, my friend …"'

Where had all this Ibsen stuff come from, had the literary meeting of minds begun, in a bar – or bed – somewhere? Con made a restless gesture, thrusting his torso forward. When he wanted to walk there was no stopping him. Very stooped, he made for the door. Spontaneously, both women took an arm each, a reluctant walk in the circumstances, all three side-by-side. The route took them round and round a central atrium. A carer looked tenderly at Con as they passed.

'Hello Uma,' Fiona said. The week before, she'd heard him patiently trying to give Con football news. From Nigeria, Uma was in Ireland for training.

'He is good today,' he said. His voice had a real positivity she admired. He wasn't just saying it; his eyes widened. He meant to reassure her. The place was full of people like Con, stumbling, mumbling, wanting – then rejecting – attention. Wasn't the vocation to care an amazing blessing?

They passed a seated area where men were gathered. Some were open-mouthed, some made sounds, others silent, all were thin. A man walked towards them, grinning. 'Christy Ring was the greatest hurler, wasn't he?' Fiona nodded. 'Christy Ring!' he repeated, his voice rising. Fiona watched Uma arrive and put his arm round the man, guiding him into a chair. When they came round on their next circuit to the same group of men, the hurling fan was silent.

Fiona spoke softly to Con as they walked, updating him on Nóra and Ciarán, the neighbours, friends who'd asked about him, bits of gossip, as if it mattered. She just kept talking, getting no reaction, always hoping for one. A sudden grunt might seem like progress of a sort. Four rounds of the corridor later they were back in Con's room. Fiona sat her husband down on a chair, leaned over, whispered something affectionate into his ear, and kissed him gently.

'Copenhagen …' he said suddenly. She glanced at the stranger, who looked unsettled.

'You must have been a little surprised to see me,' Kirsten said, as they nervously fingered coffee cups later. 'We met when he had his TV company, but I hadn't heard from him for a while, so I contacted his colleague, Pat – you know him?'

'Of course,' said Fiona, coldly.

Alarm bells were ringing. If Kirsten was a colleague, why had Con never mentioned her? She was determined to remain calm. For now.

Fiona had time to look properly at the woman now – take her in. The stranger was confident and elegantly dressed, a very calm customer. Images of Denmark, the Snow Queen, beautiful but icy, Hans Christian Andersen fairy tales, everything cool and Nordic came to mind. Her imagination was fired – so Con had a secret fairy-tale of his own.

What had he seen in her? Well, she was beautiful, for starters, and a few years younger than her. And she'd travelled a long way to look at a broken-down man and sing to him.

Someone else – another woman – had an emotional attachment to her husband. That came as a shock, even though she remembered the hotel receipt and the photo.

Distraction came when an elderly patient began a low wail that lasted several seconds. His wife looked embarrassed, but people making involuntary sounds wasn't unusual here.

Looking directly at Kirsten, she tried to keep up the conversation. 'Con and I have been married for twenty-five years.'

'I know,' was the reply. 'I am just a friend from some time ago.'

It was formal, precise-sounding English, but that didn't make it any easier to hear. Fiona found herself looking at the woman's lips, their texture, the way they moved as she spoke, her complexion and sparsely made-up face. She couldn't help imagining the two of them together and what those lips might have done with her husband, somewhere.

Kirsten put down her cup, stood up, buttoned her smart wool coat, but not before Fiona noticed her figure again. 'I must catch a flight to London. It was good to see him, but so sad. I hope I haven't intruded?'

There was silence.

'Con has been so clever and gifted,' Kirsten said, as Fiona saw a tear leave the Danish woman's eye. That was another shock. Her parting line – 'Nice to meet you' – seemed redundant.

Fiona could think of nothing to say. She took a step to follow, as if she had a question, or a tirade. But she stopped as

Kirsten got into a waiting taxi and watched as the interloper drew her legs into the car before the door closed.

Con was sleeping when she got back to the room. A bitter thought came; grand for him to look so childlike and innocent. She wanted to say to him calmly, 'By the way, I've just been told by a stranger that you're her lover. Is there something you'd like to tell me?' She'd like to ask him why Kirsten wasn't here to mind him, wash his clothes, liaise with the staff, and worry about him constantly. Pitiful thoughts and so many questions. All she could do was look at him, feeling utterly helpless and bereft. There was nowhere to take her outrage to.

Recalling Kirsten's features, she wondered what was it about her? Beautiful, or was she? She liked sex more than Fiona, maybe – and that flattered his vanity?

A family photograph on the bedside locker caught her eye, a summer holiday in France. She remembered a sleepy, pictur-esque French town that industry and youth had abandoned. It's tatty but charming bar where fellas gambled, innocently sipping pressions at all hours of the day. The small market square framed by elegant buildings, their cracked plaster no one would ever bother to repair. A woman in her late seven-ties still ran her 'Boulangerie Artisanale' with great pride. The locals seemed to live for a laidback today rather than be pres-surised with thoughts of tomorrow. Nice, that rural French culture. Decline of a different sort, but people maybe had affairs there too.

A noise from Con interrupted her thoughts. She looked in vain for some sign, new expression, but he settled back to the lost look she knew so well. What was going on in that brain? Had the stranger made an impression? Fiona could try asking him about his earlier reference to Copenhagen but decided to let the poor man sleep. She would have to deal with this new twist to their story on her own. The science reading came back, a discussion about a part of the brain she could become an expert on, the hippocampus. Con's brain was probably operating with virtually no hippocampus left, causing the loss of any ability to create new memories. He'd probably already forgotten about the stranger.

Fiona hadn't. Her own brain had a lot to process: jealousy, for starters, then musings about love, commitment, their years of marriage and so much more. It wasn't that she didn't acknowledge her own independent emotional life, desires in the past, a secret or two. How ironic, though – this woman's appearance was a reminder of the lively, engaged, adventurous man she had met twenty-six years earlier. So why be surprised his charms beguiled another? But that thought lost out heavily to jealousy – and feeling humiliated. He wouldn't be much use to anyone in a nice bed in Copenhagen now.

The phone vibrated in her bag. She looked at the screen. 'Hey! I haven't seen you around for ages. I'm cheeky, but I'll be in The Chateau later, about 5.30, if you fancy a drink?'

It was Phelim O'Sullivan. The text was a surprise; it felt a bit forward, but she could do with some normal human company. Her fingers hit the screen: 'OK. See you then.'

She felt loss and pangs of guilt about leaving Con as she stood waiting for the bus back to the city. When she took her seat and composed herself, she decided on some Googling, desperate to know more. Kirsten Frifelt seemed to be well-known in the Scandinavian TV business. On Facebook – sure enough, her smiling face appeared, a woman in a sophisticated evening dress at some gathering or other.

The sun streamed into the bus, distracting her. It seemed to highlight the harbour area in the distance, the Lee Delta as Con's friends sometimes called it, their muso-romantic hats on. Con would always go on about how it had split into two channels thousands of years ago, leaving an island between two streams, a place that was now the city's beating heart. The Liffey just cut straight through Dublin, but the Lee divides then meets again; a nice piece of resolution, she thought. She knew how an Elizabethan poet, Edmund Spenser, observed it.

The spreading Lee, that like an island fayre,
Encloseth Corke with his divided flood ...

On Lower Glanmire Road she saw a Bus Éireann advert beside Kent Station. Though she'd lived here for 25 years, Fiona could still laugh at Cork's attitude to the capital. The advertising agency knew how to exploit Cork pride: 'Bus Éireann – Bringing Dublin Closer (But not too close, like).'

By the time her bus crossed the river and rolled into the Parnell Place terminal, she'd nearly forgotten about the Kirsten woman. Rather than torment herself with further searches, she had a few minutes of a walk and was glad to put the phone away.

The calm didn't last long. 'The nerve of her!' she said, sitting at the bar a little later, a gin and tonic in front of her.

Phelim seemed amused by the whole thing. She suspected he still fancied her a bit but hoped he wouldn't come on strong – or anything like that. His approach to life always interested her: he'd taken early retirement from teaching. His semi-detached attitude to the profession led him to take off to Vietnam for two years. He'd even turned up in a YouTube clip from the local *X Factor* singing 'Johnny Don't Go to Ball-incollig,' loving the idea of amusing his friends from the other side of the globe.

He teased her. 'What was she? Good-looking I bet?'

'What's that got to do with anything?'

'A good bit,' he said – provocatively.

It was a version of flirting – by teasing her about a Scandi-navian beauty. The more Fiona railed against her, the more his curiosity about the mystery woman grew.

'I think you might have been jumping to conclusions about her and Con,' he said.

Fiona didn't tell him about the woman's startling admission. That was too personal.

'But I still bet she'd great legs?' he said, nearing the end of his second pint. 'And Nordic women tend not to be too heavy.'

As it happened, Fiona hadn't forgotten her earlier glimpse of svelte limb.

Phelim was calling the barman for more drinks when she said she'd be off. It was a Friday, so there was Choral Evensong in Saint Fin Barre's Cathedral, in the general direction of home, so she'd make a detour. She left the bar and walked down Patrick Street to Grand Parade, then down Tuckey Street. At the bottom she turned left at Ziggy's Bar and the thought that Con would never again darken the door of this place saddened her. He loved rough and ready bars, and this was one of his favourites.

Over the Lee at South Gate Bridge, she turned right onto French's Quay. The imposing Gothic revival church was close now, named after the city's patron saint of the early seventh century. Fiona had a reverence for the Anglican Church – faith was faith, she believed. (A pupil once asked, 'Miss, was St Finbarr a Protestant or a Catholic?').

A restful choral sound drifted out as the heavy door opened. The imposing interior of marble, hardwood, and stained glass were comforting to see in the fading light and calmed the turmoil of that very strange day. She picked a seat close to the ornate pulpit depicting the four Evangelists in relief. John, Matthew, Mark, and Luke were all reading intently, eyes so focused and engaged. Not like the face in that picture in the home, she thought. A line came to her from Matthew's gospel, Jesus going through all the cities and villages, proclaiming the gospel of the kingdom, and healing every disease and every affliction. There was hope in it, at least.

The choir were singing the 'Nunc dimittis' by Tomás Luis de Victoria, the sixteenth-century Spanish composer. *Si – cut – e – rat in prin – ci – pi – o* ... She knew it from a choir she'd been in, remembering the way the choirmaster, a Spaniard, could sing each part at will as he rehearsed the singers; this sacred music special for him. It was difficult to get the hang of it, but she remembered the flutter-in-the-heart feeling when the four parts came together and the singers – and everyone in the church – seemed transported.

The phone vibrated again, spoiling the solemnity, as the Latin words insisted on belief and order. She said a prayer for Con and the others in the home. The choir were close to the powerful ending. A joyous resolution:

As it was in the beginning, is now
and will be for ever

Amen.

After the day that had passed, it was consolation.

Back in the frosty night, she checked her phone. There was a text from Phelim. 'Enjoyed the drinks x'. She wasn't sure about the 'x' but would think of a response later. She was glad the other text was more straightforward – it was from Nóra.

'Mam, where are you? Dinner's ready.'

She was happy to be in mother mode again.

30

Fiona saw the outline of a regal-looking figure and the 'Danmark' stamp as she picked up the envelope. Suspecting who it had come from, her fingers' dexterity failed as they grappled with it. The writing paper had a faint perfumed scent, a disturbing trace of another. Then the handwriting intruded.

Dear Fiona,

Now that we have met briefly, I wanted to tell you what I am feeling. I was very sad to see Con that day in the hospital. I know this will have been difficult for you to accept. I understand, of course. But I feel that I should explain myself.

Is she writing to clear the air? Fiona thought of Con and Kirsten hand in hand somewhere, when she would have been innocently worrying about the kids' schoolwork, her parents' health. She read on.

So, I will begin at the beginning. We met in early 2015, at one of the TV gatherings. We got talking and were attracted to each other, really. We found each other interesting. Neither of us was seeking a new relationship. We both had responsibilities, young children. We started writing and texting each other. Who started it, you may wonder? It was Con more than me. But I didn't ask him to go away, I admit. Anyway, the contact became more and more frequent, more intimate, you could say. We both said we'd like to see each other again. An opportunity came when I had to travel to London for my work. To be honest, I think that's when we fell in love.

Who chased who? Who was most to blame? Did it even matter now? Fiona thought about the 'in love' concept; a person in love couldn't help what happened. *Bullshit!*

Con has such nice qualities. He was gentle, polite, interested in the world. He would have stimulating things to say about everything. Sorry to say this, but I loved being with him. Our last meeting was in 2017. It could be called a cooling off, in a way. But we still had some contact by SMS.

My view on the relationship was that it was not binding on either of us. We enjoyed each other's company, in every way. I don't think either of us ever thought of leaving our families. It was an excitement in our lives, to meet secretly, never for more than one night. I have a lot of mixed thoughts about the whole thing now. I sometimes think we were just selfish and, in a way, indulgent.

Then I think, was it wrong if nobody knew about it? We weren't hurting anyone. It was love.

Does that mean you were both helpless? Is this some kind of therapy for you? More sad than angry, she kept reading.

It was infatuation, you might say, as you read this. Perhaps I am just making some excuses for my behaviour. I have been having a strong sex drive, I think. It has caused me to think less about the consequences of infidelity. The truth is I risked a lot to be with Con. Last year, my husband found out about the whole thing when he saw a message on my phone. Our marriage has never been the same.

I always said to Con that he had to look after his own life, his own conscience. He wasn't obliged to keep meeting me, having sex with me. And for me it was the same. And we never discussed our partners or said bad things about them. On this point I can assure you.

Stop repeating yourself! But impatience with the writer didn't stop, the word 'sex' getting Fiona's imagination working. What was it about making love with her that he liked so much that he didn't care for with me? He must have compared us. She became conscious of her body, involuntarily adjusting a bra strap.

I don't like to call it an affair, but I know that is what it was. I came to see him in the hospital because I felt I had to. I knew I might meet you and I planned to say we were just professional colleagues. But I felt so sad to see him like that that I couldn't help myself and so I told the truth.

You might think, how dare I grieve for someone else's husband? But I must ask you, can you accept the idea that the memory of Con as a fully healthy, energetic person will be shared by both of us?

Sincerely,
Kirsten (Frifelt)

Why end a letter with a provocative question like that? This woman was taking some indulgent liberties with another person's marriage, inserting herself where she wasn't wanted. Fiona felt wounded and angry. The suggestion that they'd 'share' Con was brazen. But the person she was effectively mourning wasn't an innocent party either. He wasn't led astray, he bought in, made secret arrangements, and travelled distances to meet with this person. His betrayal made a lie of everything, the years of togetherness and commitment to her and the kids, their whole time together really, all the time indulging a selfish other life. It was eating her up. *Words, words, words,* she thought, wiping a tear.

The school year had ended. She was trying to put some order on her turbulent life. She made several visits to their doctor, thinking it an odd twist of fate to be sitting in the same surgery discussing *her* mental fogginess, remembering Con's helpless look sitting here only two years earlier. Now it was her brain that was at issue.

'It's normally protected by a surrounding layer of spinal fluid, but if the brain is suddenly jarred, it may bounce or twist inside the skull, resulting in concussion,' the doctor said. He felt her skull with gentle, warm fingers. 'It can be serious, Fiona,' he said. 'You could experience memory problems.'

She glanced around the room, noticing a painting propped against the wall: no one had found the time to hang it. The view was of Clew Bay with Croagh Patrick in the distance.

'It's my daughter's painting,' he said.

'It brings back memories,' Fiona said.

The day with her mother on that mountain was vivid. It brought a dull ache to her chest.

'Feeling emotional is common with concussion,' he continued.

Fiona just stared at the painting. She thought of her mother's vulnerability, her grace, her smile. Then an antiseptic smell brought her back to the room, the doctor, surgery, advice, medicine.

'Let me know how you're getting on before the end of the week?' he said.

She was still thinking about memory as the car inched through city-centre traffic, before climbing the hill towards her new reality, the care home. Sympathetic nods would be exchanged with other spouses, all of them in the same boat, a kind of community forged from desperate necessity. Staff did their best to keep the mood positive and as upbeat as it could be in a place like this. Then there'd be Con in his room; all helpless – innocent. But the Kirsten letter left a sick feeling in the pit of her stomach that wouldn't go away.

It didn't stop her sitting by the bed, slowly caressing his fingers, as he lay curled up in the foetal position. Uma told her this happens with the disease. She wondered about that once-lively brain; what messages, if any, were being transmitted now? Had the highway of his nervous system become a pileup, things crashing into other things – carnage?

Curious thoughts kept intruding – worry about *herself* now. A kind of delirium had set in – was the concussion having an effect? She saw a scene at the Gates of Paradise: Con being greeted by serene-looking angels and a huge choir like in Mahler's *Symphony of a Thousand*, only for the great cacophony of that work to fade suddenly. Saint Peter stood looking stern: 'Con from Cork, is it? What about this woman, Kirsten, Con? You weren't straight with the people who trusted you and cared about you most?'

Fiona's conscience was prodded by a realisation of deceit on her part too. Con would go to his eternal reward not knowing about a crucial part of her past and sensing her meeting in Athlone wasn't what she claimed it to be. Why hadn't she come clean with him, before his brain began to deteriorate? Her head was splitting again. Was the pain more karma?

Family photos arranged around the room offered something to cling to. Images of happy times – a sudden kiss in the swimming pool in a holiday house in France, their first drink at the gig in 1993, the shared joy of Ciarán and Nóra, the tender moments in Clare and Kerry, knowing his mental powers were fading. All that contentment couldn't all have been a lie, could it?

'Con, remember our holiday in the Loire?'

Empty eyes stared at her.

'You nearly drowned one day.'

He let out a loud sigh.

'And you loved the colourful balloons floating across the sky. You found them so inspiring, didn't you? Last night, Nóra and Ciarán were talking about the first night you brought them to the Corner House for drinks? Apparently, you kept ordering more, saying "a bird never flew on one wing". They didn't know what to make of it.'

That week, she had a difficult discussion with Pat Roche, his draft script in front of him. The mental strain continued, a feeling of near indifference as he described how strange it felt to be spooling the material, his friend and associate moving helplessly back and forth, at speed, with a chipmunk voice. But he wanted to go ahead and get to air. This was business.

'But Con is still alive, Pat,' she pleaded.

'It might make the programme more effective.'

It was his professional dispassion that hurt her. 'Hadn't Con pictured this scenario?' he said, attempting to placate her.

'Really?'

'Yes. I felt I heard him saying, "You're on to something there, boi. Keep it going."'

Fiona was on edge the day she watched a rough cut of the programme, a healthier Con haunting the pictures. Impressionistic shots of the river, blurred streetscapes, the hills above the city, pub interiors, the shaky camerawork, deliberately shifting in and out of focus. It ended with a Ger Wolfe song, about darkness.

It's all dark, it's but the night, child,
It has its own light, when all the day is fast asleep,
And it's so quiet, it is but silence,
It has its own song, when all the birds are gone away.

'But Pat, Con's still with us,' she tried again, a lump in her throat.

'You see, the point is that even in darkness there can be promise,' he said, looking pleased that his philosophising might mollify her. Tears welled up and she didn't respond. He asked her to watch another section of footage he hadn't used. Con had recorded it late one night, sounding upset, his words garbled, holding a framed photo of her and the kids as he spoke.

'I … I think Fiona hasn't told me about something in her past. America and that fella, James. That must have been what … what the time in … Athlone was about … she was meeting *him …*'

A whisky bottle was visible in the shot. Con held a glass and seemed all over the place, slobbering. 'Feck you, Pat! You'll be getting praise for the programme, drinking pints, and I'll be just mumbling, if I make any sound at all. No. Your guinea pig has had enough ...'

Fiona was upset now. 'And yet that day when he disappeared, he'd gone out with the camera ...?'

'A real pro,' Pat said.

'Your experiment, Pat. Con wanted to oblige you. And what happened to the footage found in the water?' she asked, thinking it might be better if the memory card been left to rust away at the bottom of the Lee.

'Con was talking in a pub about ...' He stopped. 'Ah ... the footage was ropey, Con was mostly out of shot, so I put in a piece of you saying, "As the disease got worse, he really didn't know truth from fantasy."'

'I see,' she said quietly, trying to hide her anger. Is this what media people can be like – callous, cavalier with other peoples' lives? she wondered.

Phelim O'Sullivan invited her for coffee after the programme was broadcast. They sat together in a small café, aromatic coffee smells wafting through the Art Deco-inspired arcade, it's elegant copper window frames carefully polished. He delivered well-embellished news, with the trademark sarcasm she remembered from the staff room. His companionship – and the complications it might bring – crossed her mind. After one of his clever gags, she felt inclined to lean across and squeeze his arm but decided not to. Phelim could be an emotional handful, she suspected, when out of devil-may-care mode, so she didn't want to send mixed signals.

'Nice to see you and have a chat. I don't know whether I'm coming or going these days,' she said, as they parted on Oliver Plunkett Street. Her tone might have been a little cold, she thought – friendships mattered. A few yards on, she looked back and caught him smiling after her. They exchanged waves.

Deirdre got in touch to say that she and Pauline had split up. Fortunately, she'd kept her little house in Dublin, and was back there. 'You should come and visit sometime soon.'

Would Deirdre come on strong again – she couldn't handle another drama right now. She'd let that one sit. A lot of time had passed since that night in Dublin; doubts planted about her own sexuality a distant memory now. She didn't think she'd see radiance in Deirdre's countenance again like that day in Bewley's all those years ago. Instead, Deirdre was a woman like herself, with baggage, both on a journey towards old age.

One evening, she couldn't resist taking Kirsten's letter out again, drawn to it in a morbid kind of way, allowing the paper, the stranger's handwriting, to disturb her again. She went to the fridge for a glass of wine, a Touraine she liked.

Maybe I should reply, she decided after a soothing sip. I might appear vulnerable and pathetic to her if I don't. I'll be the better person here, be strong instead, after all, I did nothing wrong. Glass in hand she went out to the back garden. Getting dark now, the evening was warm and the sky clear, stars coming out, getting more visible. The city's glow and muted sounds in the distance formed the backdrop. She thought of the day she'd first come here; the places Con had proudly shown her. He wanted her to love Cork. She struggled to blot out thoughts of Con and Kirsten wrapped around each other, their kissing and intimacy all heightened by their stealth. He was infatuated, and, like a lot of men, easily flattered.

She went back to the fridge, poured another glass of wine, opened her laptop, and started to type.

Dear Kirsten,

Then she deleted 'dear.'

You have asked me to, as you put it, 'share the memory' of Con. At first, that made me angry.

She heard the front door. Nóra came bounding in from choir practice. 'Hi Mam. What are you up to?'

Fiona looked wearily at her. 'Something I have to do, a bit of unfinished business – from your dad's life.'

Nóra clearly couldn't think of a response. 'Well, I'm off to bed.' She looked at the full glass and smiled. 'Easy on the ol' vino, Mam?'

Silence returned and Fiona tapped the keys again.

To be honest, it's hard not to think of you as an enemy. But I have been trying to look at the situation as rationally as I can. So, I must admit that he was, to some extent, a part of your life. But he loved me; I know that. Can you love two people at the same time? I say no, it sounds a bit too convenient.

Then I look at it another way; you're the person who makes a lie of so much of what I shared with my husband. That's all water under the bridge, as we call it, but fidelity is a concept I believe in. I'm a little old-fashioned.

She was hitting the keys with venom when the kitchen door opened.

'You still up?' Nóra said, pouring herself a large glass of water before tiptoeing away.

Fiona banished the thought of confiding in her daughter. Leave well enough alone; her father could do no wrong, so why disillusion her now. Sooner or later, she'd have a day in the dock – their secret half-sister revealed – with all the questions it would raise about their mother.

She typed again.

There were too many good things about our life together, great memories that make it hard not to forgive him. I loved Con. I made a commitment to him when we got married. He did the same for me. Then he broke those vows with you. I can't escape that fact. Maybe it was just physical, maybe not. I looked at him in the home that day you were there and wanted to hit him, a defenceless invalid, because he had sex with you …

She paused and took a large sip of wine. A confessional thought came: what about the little person – her own flesh and blood – that she never gave a chance to love her all those years ago?

I'm over it. Anyway, you've admitted the passion faded. And he didn't desert his family.

Keep it short, she decided; give no cause for a debate about what was done and dusted. She put down the empty glass. But it wasn't the end of it. She sat at the table as the night wore on. Then her mood changed. It may have been the wine. She decided that she was being a bit too compliant with Kirsten. She took the cursor to what she'd written and watched with satisfaction as it ate through the words she'd deliberated on not long before. Why should I acquiesce to the betrayal of my marriage? She began to type again.

I hope, I really hope, you are not looking for some forgiveness, or some justification for the betrayal of your own marriage vows, your indulgence with my husband?

Yes, this was the right tone, she decided.

Whatever Con felt for you was probably the result of his illness. You know this disease can be in a person's brain many years before it's diagnosed. To call it a love affair is really pushing it.

She wasn't sure she believed this and had to stop to wipe tears from the keyboard.

I'm sure you noticed odd behaviour on the occasions you met. I refuse to believe you didn't. But you didn't care.

She was getting angry, making noise with the keys, fighting with the alphabet in front of her, so she stopped. She wasn't even sure she believed what she'd written. Two letters, two realities, two different views of personal histories. It was the dead of night. She thought of all the loves and losses, the dreams, the hopes, the betrayals that sleep was pausing across the city now, across the world.

Something else plagued her mind: a thing Lily had revealed at their second meeting, a month before.

'I did some investigating into my dad,' Lily announced. Fiona wasn't surprised, but it still caused a little tremor. Lily took a photo out of her bag. It was a picture of a bearded man beside a pickup truck, a rifle in his hand, arid countryside behind him. Fiona thought she recognised the features. She felt a strange sensation, that the past was a huge tornado swirling across open country towards her, and she was powerless to stop it. 'It took a lot of tracking down to get that. I'd very little to go on, except a very unusual surname.' She looked across at the photo that Fiona placed on the table.

'He died ten years ago. He'd ended up in the middle of Arizona, a hard-drinking loner, it seems, in a small community in the desert. I found the place on Google Maps, about sixty or seventy miles from Phoenix.' She let out a nervous chuckle. 'Lots of highway and the odd cactus. I think I spotted his local; the stars and stripes on a pole beside a clapboard place, a couple of men sitting on a veranda with beers, frozen in time by Google, really. The street view is amazing, isn't it?'

James – who had become Jim – met someone from a religious cult a few years before. American life, the open spaces, the promise of something or other seduced him, and he'd avoided any visa issues by marrying. There'd only been sporadic contact between him and his family in Dublin, Lily told her. When Fiona had revealed the unusual surname a few months before, it wasn't too difficult for Lily to find the family. His parents had given up on their son; a drifter in the American West wasn't their idea of achievement. Fiona imagined an elderly couple with no financial worries, but lonely in their Dublin mansion – he'd probably broken their hearts. She pictured the room where she'd first gone to bed with James all those years ago, perhaps now decked with cobwebs, his Blues posters probably well-yellowed. Lily was nothing if not intrepid and, God love her, she needed and deserved to know.

Fiona looked again at the face in the photo, an intimate stranger. That was the shocking part; the product of her union with him, now sitting opposite her and she a stranger too. Fiona though in Biblical terms: you will reap what you sow. She remembered when she was in love with James, her first real love, his impish smile captured in a moment and looking back at her down the years. He could be striding across the cobbles of Trinity College still. She saw his long fingers pluck guitar strings and heard his voice. It was loud but not sweet and echoed uncomfortably around her head. James seemed to stare intensely at her from this photo, a disturbing echo from another part of her life.

'He must have adapted to life there among the cacti. He looks like one of those Trump supporters,' she joked.

Lily didn't appreciate the attempt at levity. Fiona felt her posture go rigid again; this was the father of the beautiful woman sitting on the other side of the table. For some reason, she imagined the classic grave from the Western films, the mound of earth with a simple wooden cross, maybe tumbleweeds rolling by the plot. She thought of Mississippi, the Tallahatchie Bridge she never got to, the night she lay awake, the careless conception confirmed (the hotel's bedside table legs made with deer limbs seemed grotesque), before composing herself.

'He can only have been about forty-nine or so? So sad. May God rest him.' The invocation made Lily look away.

'Imagine an elderly couple, in the twilight of their lives, who hadn't experienced the joy of being grandparents – till now?' Lily said.

They'd told her their story, a son, heartbroken, when Fiona left him in America. He'd drifted, then heard from college friends about the pregnancy and wrote to Fiona saying he wanted to come home for the birth and patch things up.

Fiona knew she'd have to live with Lily's unease at that version of events. Was memory playing tricks on Fiona, or had she bent recall to *her* narrative? Life's clouds and illusions, she thought – don't we all rewrite events, edit and re-edit scenes? But no; she wasn't imagining the unpleasantness of that time.

Would her story and Lily's be like a film with one of those sad, happy endings?

She took another of the pills the doctor had prescribed. Sighing more than once, she paced up and down, then decided: she would draw a line under the whole thing, send neither of the letters, nor any other. They couldn't express her true feelings and why dress up how shattered she felt? Anyway, karma had come to that household in Denmark – wasn't it in the letter? Kirsten got a comeuppance of sorts. That was enough. Karma, she liked the word, a belief from another faith brought solace.

Time for sleep, but then something else occurred to her: an idea to complete a section of her memoir. Her fingers were back to the keyboard – to close another chapter.

The last morning – a Mississippi sky loaded up with greys. My mind could summon the hollers, the twanging strings eking out emotions. My soul was drawn to the music, but my heart and body had taken a pounding – this landscape of myth tarnished by my fellow traveller. I might be back. But for now, let the ghosts play their blues. I was going home.

Closing the tab, she rubbed her eyes as the icons disappeared. Her head was hurting again. She was on her way to bed as the last signs of life left the screen.

31

Incense filled the air in Christ the King Church, a coda to the Requiem Mass. Nóra looked at Ciarán and Máirín, stood up from the pew and started to walk, pausing in front of the altar, glancing at the coffin. The piece of paper in her hand was shaking as she stopped at the lectern. Another tear fell on the already smudged words, and she began.

'It's been a difficult time for our family. We always knew this terrible disease existed. We found ourselves having to study it, get to know it, because it was ravaging our family. Ciarán and I watched our parents trying so hard to keep their relationship alive through terrible times. My mother battling to keep our dad present, with us. He could be so difficult. It was sometimes hard to remember the loving, carefree man he once was, the great father he worked hard to be. The disease has been described as a slow fade to black. Yet my dad never gave up hope, the hope of a miracle … remission, of course, it never came. At least the world knows that it's a disease; for years people were condemned for being senile.

So, we knew about the inevitable; that our dear father would die. But we couldn't have imagined last week's turn of events. Our mother, Fiona, gave Dad so much care. Too much, as it turned out. She was a wonderful woman, mother, and wife. A Dubliner born and bred, she came to Cork to make a life here with my dad and grew to love it.

She brought a passion for literature and art into her teaching work. Ciarán and I often met kids our age who would praise Mrs Twomey. And some were tough kids, too. We felt proud, Mam.

Whether it came from faith or somewhere else, Mam believed in other realities. She liked repeating a line from Hamlet: 'There are more things in heaven and earth, Horatio, than are dreamt of in your philosophy.' In another life, I think she would have been a successful writer.

This church has held a special place in her heart since her move south in 1994, to start a new phase of her life with my father. Recently, it became an oasis from the troubles that befell her. We had to deal with a secret she'd kept for 35 years, discovered by accident in an innocent phone call from a half-sister we knew nothing about. Now, we may never know why she didn't share it with us. I suppose we all have our secrets. And Mam had hers.'

She looked at the sea of faces trained on her, all listening intently to the words choking her. She recognised most people, then fixed her gaze on a woman near the front who caught her eye. The resemblance was uncanny; she could be looking at her mother's ghost. It was the features, and the way this person held herself.

They had only spoken by phone. There would be a lot to talk about when this day was over. Nóra felt elation, and shock, but Lily's smile encouraged her to go on.

'The tragedy that ended Mam's life so suddenly was the result of caring, and that's a small consolation. As you may know, violent incidents can be a part of the later stages of Alzheimer's. I remember her shock the night it happened, but she seemed to make a recovery, or so we thought. The incident that damaged her felt like a betrayal by my dad. I know it did, but I also know she loved him and forgave his actions. She knew it was the disease and not him. Her concussion didn't seem too worrying, little did we know. Pain and headaches from the trauma never went away. She hit her head when she slipped on the street and complications set in. Our wonderful, inspiring Mam just slipped away from us ...'

Outside the church, Nóra invited Lily to stand with her, Máirín and Ciarán as people offered condolences. Watching her half-sister shed tears, for a mother she'd never known, made the day seem even more surreal.

Still in a daze that afternoon, she sat indifferent as the bus swayed and bumped its way to St Malachy's. Staff members nodded to her on the familiar corridors. Uma told her it was time to blow out the candle he'd lit at the bedside, to coincide with the funeral. Con was dozing on the bed as she pulled up a chair.

'Dad … we gave Mam a good send-off today. The church was full. It was a lovely Mass.'

Con sighed involuntarily. Tears rolled down Nóra's face, smudging her mascara again. 'I shook so many hands, people who said lovely things about Mam.'

Music wafted from a CD player, playing in case it might register with him; Van Morrison singing, unheeded, about soul and spirit on a journey.

'Dad … wait till I tell you …' She held up her finger with a bright new ring on it. 'I'm engaged!'

She waited in vain for a reaction. 'Guess what? His name is Rory. He lives near us. He's a Callaghan, from St Patrick's Road. He really likes music, not so much your kind, Dad … but you never know …?'

She couldn't hold back the tears now. 'Mam met him. She really, really liked him. I know she did. He was at the station the day we went to see the pope.'

Her father's eyes opened a little.

'Dad, I think he's special. I know we can be happy together.'

She heard sounds from the corridor, a shout, a cry, soothing words; another flare-up being managed.

'I'd better go now, Dad. I'm going over to Rory's house.'

She thought she heard him make a faint sound.

'Dad. You know I love you?' she said.

She stood listening, watching the candle, imagining her mother, not in the cold earth of a suburban cemetery, but looking radiant, somewhere. The light flickered for the last time when she gently aimed her breath at the flame.

Acknowledgements

I'm grateful to many people who helped shape this book: early steers came from my son, Rory. Paula Elmore and Mary Rose Callaghan gave encouraging feedback. My wife, Carol Louthe, made pivotal observations at a crucial stage. Alison Walsh's great editorial skills brought transformative suggestions to later drafts.

Others inspired or helped in different ways: Dave McHugh, Tim Lehane, Stina Greaker, Seán Farrell, Colm O'Callaghan, Pia Maria Marquard, the late Kevin Linehan, Dr Michael O'Tighearnaigh, Aoife Maher, John Healy, Jerry O'Reilly, the *Irish Examiner*, and Robbie McGrane and Maggie Dooney of Little Gem Tours for the opportunity to rediscover the west of Ireland.

I'm grateful to songwriters who kindly gave permission to quote from their work: Ger Wolfe for 'The Lark of Mayfield' and 'It's All Dark'; John Spillane for 'Let the River Flow'. Lines by Pearse Hutchinson from *At Least for a While* (2008) reproduced by kind permission of the estate of the author and The Gallery Press. Lines from Paul O'Brien's ballad, 'The Shovels Number Nine' is reproduced by permission of the author.

I'm indebted to Rita Bowen for advice on adoption law and procedure in Ireland. Several works on Alzheimer's Disease were of assistance, including *The Forgetting*, David Shenk; *Married to Alzheimer's*, Steph Booth; *Alzheimer's Disease Decoded*, Ronald Sahyouni; *Somebody I Used to Know*, Wendy Mitchell; also, *On the Blues Trail – Travels in America*, by Paul Outhwaite.

Finally, I greatly appreciate the encouragement of Michael Brennan, Eileen O'Brien and Kerstin Mierke at Orpen Press.